M000013552

THE DEVIL'S BLAZE

Also by Robert J. Harris

The Thirty-One Kings
Castle Macnab
A Study in Crimson

SHERLOCK HOLMES 1943

ROBERT J. HARRIS

PEGASUS CRIME
NEW YORK LONDON

THE DEVIL'S BLAZE

Pegasus Crime is an imprint of
Pegasus Books, Ltd.
148 West 37th Street, 13th Floor
New York, NY 10018

First Pegasus Books cloth edition November 2022

ISBN: 978-1-63936-248-6

10 9 8 7 6 5 4 3 2 1

Printed in the United States of America
Distributed by Simon & Schuster
www.pegasusbooks.com

To Robert and Hazel –
'You have been in Bahrain, I perceive.'

CONTENTS

PART THREE: REICHENBACH

PREFACE

Following two successful Victorian-set Sherlock Holmes films produced by 20th Century Fox, which starred Basil Rathbone and Nigel Bruce, the Holmes franchise was taken over by Universal Pictures. The two actors were by now so well established in their roles as Holmes and Watson that the studio felt they could take the bold step of updating the characters to 1942 in *Sherlock Holmes and the Voice of Terror*. This was the first of a series of twelve very popular 1940s-set adventures that confirmed Basil Rathbone as the definitive Sherlock Holmes. These films inspired me to reimagine this version of the great detective in my novel *A Study in Crimson*, which sent him in pursuit of a ruthless killer in the blacked-out streets of wartime London. This tale was warmly received and it was clear to me that there was another story yet to be told. The second film in the series, *Sherlock Holmes and the Secret Weapon*, featured the veteran actor Lionel Atwill as Holmes's nemesis, Professor Moriarty. I saw here an opportunity to reimagine this classic confrontation against the background of World War II, with Atwill's performance in mind. Also, as in my first novel, Inspector Lestrade and Mrs Hudson are presented as they were portrayed by Dennis Hoey and Mary Gordon in the film series. As is so often the case, Holmes and Watson await us in the comfortable surroundings of Baker Street. They have at this point no suspicion that they are about to be hurled into the most dangerous adventure of their careers.

It lies with me to tell for the first time what really took place between Professor Moriarty and Mr Sherlock Holmes.

The Final Problem
SIR ARTHUR CONAN DOYLE

PART ONE

INFERNO

1

THE VANISHING VAMPIRE

It was with some relief that I welcomed Inspector Lestrade and his two companions into our Baker Street rooms that afternoon. Since settling the matter of the killer who called himself Crimson Jack, there had been little to satisfy Sherlock Holmes's restless intellect. Our pursuit of that murderer had occupied us from September to October of 1942, but now it was May of the following year and, while war raged across the globe, our lives had settled into a wearisome routine.

The cases that had come our way, such as the Phantom of the Underground and the Mystery of Gulliver Lodge, Holmes had disposed of with a rapidity that both amazed and disappointed me. As correct as his ingenious solutions proved to be, they did little to exercise his highly developed faculties of observation and deduction. This left him with sufficient leisure to master a number of challenging violin pieces as well as attending several of the free lunchtime concerts at the National Gallery organised by Miss Myra Hess, herself an accomplished musician. The end result, though, was that he had settled into a sort of restive ennui from which it was difficult to shake him.

Inspector Lestrade's phone call, however, promised some serious matter to engage my friend's attention. I gathered from his brief preview that the crime was a violent robbery and involved a painting, the subject matter of which had been altered in some inexplicable fashion. I found myself intrigued, but when I relayed these snippets to Holmes he barely raised his eyes from the leather-bound copy of Bede's *Ecclesiastical History of the English People* that lay open in his lap.

'I say, Holmes, do show some interest,' I remonstrated. 'Violence, robbery and the mysterious transmutation of a painting – surely these are the elements of a classic affair.'

He slowly turned the page and addressed me without looking up. 'Watson, I detect in your tone a certain eagerness for anything that will provide you with material for another of those colourful tales you will not desist from writing.'

'That at least would be better employment than watching you wallow in this unproductive lethargy,' I countered sharply.

Holmes raised a sardonic eyebrow. 'Really, Watson, I cannot help but note that a certain tetchiness has crept into your character since your friend Miss Preston returned to the United States.'

I found myself quite taken aback by his unexpected reprimand, as though he had spotted in me a symptom of some serious malady that I myself had failed to detect. 'Tetchiness? Do you think so?'

He waved a finger in the air as though to summon up the scene. 'Why, just the other day you remonstrated with Mrs Hudson quite strongly over the condition of your breakfast egg.'

'It was definitely runny . . .' I began. Then realising how petulant this sounded, I stopped myself from going any further and admitted with a sigh, 'I suppose you're right, Holmes. I apologise if I have been in any way difficult.'

'Not at all, old fellow. For years you have tolerated my idiosyncrasies with admirable good humour. And I do not blame you at all for feeling the absence of that lady as keenly as you do.'

During our pursuit of Crimson Jack I had formed a close friendship with Miss Gail Preston, an American radio journalist, whose involvement had proved crucial to the case. It was a closeness I had never expected to find again after losing my dear Mary years before and it was a hard blow when she was summoned back to the United States by her employers, the NBC radio network.

'I suppose all of us must answer the call of duty in our own way,' I said resignedly.

'Indeed,' said Holmes, who had answered that call himself many times. 'No doubt the talks she is delivering to her fellow citizens on her first-hand experiences of the conflict in Europe will prove a great boon to the war bonds drive on which she is engaged.'

'And until she returns, Holmes,' I said, steering us back to the subject at hand, 'I confess that I shall be grateful for any measure of distraction our old friend Lestrade can provide.'

Holmes did not rise to my lure, however, and returned to his reading.

Fortunately we had not much longer to wait before we heard the inspector's familiar heavy tread on the stairs. Holmes answered his knock with a summons to enter. Dressed in a tweed overcoat and his usual bowler hat, Lestrade with his broad shoulders almost entirely obscured the slight figure in the grey suit who followed him. Also in tow was a stout mustachioed fellow who owned the flushed cheeks of a country policeman. Lestrade introduced his companions as Mr Winslow Bastable and Detective Sergeant Oliver Pole, both from the village of Cobblestone in Kent.

Once they were seated, the policemen on the capacious leather settee, Bastable in a rattan chair, Holmes closed his book and set it aside.

'Well, Lestrade, from what Dr Watson has repeated to me of your telephone call, this appears to be a very standard robbery.'

'Standard it may be,' said Bastable in a thin, trembling voice, 'but in the course of this robbery my uncle Junius was violently assaulted and currently lies in a state of unconsciousness.'

'I did not intend to minimise your personal tragedy,' Holmes assured the young man, 'but serious as the matter is, such cases are not brought to me unless they exhibit one or two features of more than usual interest.'

'More than usual?' Pole expostulated. 'They are downright flabbergasting! In all my days I never heard of such a thing!'

Holmes's lip twitched uncomfortably at the outburst. Lestrade leaned forward with a serious frown, as though apologising for his colleague's excessive enthusiasm. 'I think it would be best, Oliver, if we let Mr Bastable lay out the background to the case.'

'It would, it would,' Pole agreed expansively. 'Go ahead, Mr Bastable, you tell the great detective all about it and we'll see what he makes of your extraordinary tale.'

I had the impression that this simple rustic officer had never dealt with any but the most prosaic of crimes, and that he had imposed upon Lestrade's friendship with Sherlock Holmes to bring this incident to Baker Street, like a proud angler showing off a prize catch.

Bastable nervously fingered the fair moustache that barely made its presence felt on his upper lip, then began his account of the incident.

'I am one of a small family, Mr Holmes, all of whom have lived for many years under the most humble of circumstances, and since the war have found life even more restricted. I was aware only in the vaguest way that I had an uncle Randolph Bastable, who years ago had emigrated to America where he made himself a fortune in the cotton trade. Part of his acquired wealth he used to purchase a substantial country house just outside the village of Cobblestone in Kent, taking up residence there some time in the early 1930s.

'I had never met my uncle Randolph and was consequently very surprised to be contacted by his lawyer upon his death two weeks ago. It seems that having never married and produced offspring of his own, he desired to pass on some benefit of his success to other family members bearing the name Bastable. These consisted of myself, my wife Lily, my cousins James, Herbert and Clarice, and my uncle Junius.

'We were invited to come and live together in his country house, which he had named The Poplars. There was adequate space for us each to have a private suite of rooms and, while we lived there, we would be entitled to a handsome stipend paid out of my uncle's many investments. None of us had ever imagined living in a place as grand as The Poplars and for Lily and myself it was as though we had been cast into some romantic dream.

'Among the conditions attaching to the will was that we should all move into the house on the same date, and that was agreed upon as the eighteenth of this month.'

'Just yesterday,' I mused, surprised that tragedy should have struck so quickly.

'We all knew each other only from meeting at funerals and the odd wedding, but everyone seemed equally pleased at the arrangement, as it removed the necessity of paying rent and came with a handsome income. We each moved into our own suite and sat down last night to an excellent supper provided by outside caterers.'

'The house has no servants?' Holmes inquired.

'My uncle was cared for by an elderly couple named Weeks who served as caretaker and cook. He made provision in his will for them to retire to a cottage in Cornwall, which had long been their desire, along with a modest pension as thanks for their faithful service. By the time we all arrived at the house they were long gone. They left behind a letter written by my uncle, in a sealed envelope which was to be opened by the most senior of the new residents, this being, of course, my uncle Junius, a retired fishmonger.

'Seated at the head of the table, my uncle opened the letter and read it silently to himself. I saw his eyes grow wide, but when I inquired as to the contents, he merely replied, "All in good time," and tucked it away in an inside pocket of his jacket. We were all so delighted at our new station in life that none of us was inclined to press him on the matter. For all we knew it was merely a set of instructions for tending the boiler and contacting the local laundry.'

'But in fact it was a message of the most vital importance,' Pole interjected.

'Really, Oliver, you must let Mr Bastable tell the story at his own pace,' Lestrade remonstrated.

'As you can imagine,' Bastable went on, 'with this change of circumstances, I was in such a state of excitement that I found it difficult to sleep. Leaving my wife to her slumbers, I put on my dressing gown and slippers and set off for the kitchen, intending to make myself a soothing cup of cocoa.'

'What time was this?' asked Holmes.

'According to the clock in our bedroom it was shortly after midnight,' Bastable replied. 'I made my way downstairs quietly in order not to disturb anyone else, switching on the lights as I went. Being unfamiliar with the house, I took a wrong turning in my search for the kitchen and found myself in the east wing where a light had already been switched on in the passage ahead of me. This ended in a blank wall. However, there was on the right-hand side, a few yards ahead of me, another passage which I could tell was also lit.

'Wondering who else might be abroad at this hour, I called out, "Hello, is anybody there?" Turning into the side passage, which was some twenty feet in length, I saw at the far end a figure lying on the floor below a wall safe which gaped open. It had evidently been concealed by an embroidered hanging that was pushed off to one side and was held back by the open door.

'Rushing to assist the fallen figure, I saw at once that it was my uncle Junius and that there was a patch of blood on the back of his head. In his hand he clutched what proved to be the mysterious letter from Uncle Randolph. I tried to rouse Uncle Junius, but without success as I have had no medical training. Accordingly I hastened back into the main part of the house and struck the dinner gong loudly and repeatedly to rouse the rest of the family. Once we were all gathered, James and Herbert carried my uncle up to his room and laid him on his bed where my cousin Clarice bandaged his injury. I in the meantime telephoned for the police and a doctor.'

'The painting,' Pole egged on the witness, 'the painting.'

After only a brief hesitation, Bastable complied. 'I recall quite clearly, as I rushed down the passage towards the stricken form of my uncle, noticing on my left a deep alcove. From the corner of my eye I glimpsed a painting hanging on the alcove wall that faced me as I passed.'

'I fail to see anything extraordinary in that,' said Holmes, barely suppressing a sigh.

'This was no ordinary painting, Mr Holmes,' Pole declared as majestically as a magician about to produce a dove from his kerchief. 'You tell him, Mr Bastable.'

'Well, it was a very unusual painting,' said Bastable, 'like no other in the house.' He glanced anxiously at Holmes and myself as though anticipating scepticism. 'Gentlemen, it was a portrait of a vampire.'

'A vampire?' I echoed incredulously.

'Count Dracula himself, I should say,' Bastable expanded, 'as portrayed by Bela Lugosi in the famous film.'

I saw Holmes's eyes widen the merest fraction, a sure sign that his interest had been engaged.

'That is not even the best part,' enthused Detective Sergeant Pole, barely resisting a tasteless chuckle. 'Tell him the rest, Mr Bastable!'

'Well, this morning,' Bastable continued with mounting excitement, 'when the police arrived and we examined the scene of the crime, to my utter amazement, that painting had vanished and been replaced by another.'

2

THE GIRL WITH THE YELLOW ROSE

'Are you quite sure it is not the same painting?' Holmes inquired mildly.

'Last night, Mr Holmes, it was a portrait of incarnate evil in all its horror,' Bastable insisted. 'This morning what hangs there is a young girl dressed in blue holding a yellow rose. It even bears the title plate *Girl with a Yellow Rose* by James Jebusa Shannon.'

'Yes, it hardly seems you could have mistaken one for the other,' Holmes agreed.

'By way of confirmation,' said Pole, 'I must tell you that this new painting is not even the same size and shape as the other.'

'Yes, Dracula's portrait was in an oval frame,' said Bastable, 'while the painting of the girl is in a more standard rectangular frame.'

'This is confirmed by the discoloration on the wall,' said Pole. 'I suppose you are aware, Mr Holmes, that when a painting is removed, the outline of the frame is still visible on the wallpaper.'

'Yes, I was aware of that, thank you,' Holmes responded brusquely. 'And has Mr Junius Bastable been able to speak at all?'

'No, Mr Holmes,' Bastable answered dolefully. 'He is in a state of unconsciousness and may remain so for some time.'

'It is clear that Mr Junius Bastable was struck directly on the back of the head while examining the contents of the safe,' said Detective Sergeant Pole. 'Lying on the floor was a marble figurine of a wood nymph which was clearly the weapon. It had been lifted from a nearby shelf, its position there being clear from the absence of dust.'

'Were there any fingerprints?' I asked.

'None,' said Pole. 'The attacker either wore gloves, wrapped a kerchief around the figurine, or wiped it clean of prints after the attack.'

'As he was struck suddenly from behind,' Holmes surmised, 'even if he should wake, it is unlikely that Mr Junius Bastable will be able to identify his attacker. And what exactly were the contents of the safe?'

'According to the letter left by Uncle Randolph,' said Bastable, 'a bag containing a quantity of precious jewels worth a considerable sum.'

'Said bag of jewels is, of course, missing,' Pole interjected.

'They were to be entrusted to the most senior family member,' Bastable continued, 'who would supervise their fair distribution among the others. The letter also described the location of the safe and gave the combination.'

'We may then reconstruct Uncle Junius's actions,' said Holmes. 'Reading the letter over dinner, he decided not to reveal its contents until he had confirmed the truth of it. Waiting until everyone was asleep, he rose from his bed and made his way to the safe's hidden location. Drawing aside the cover of the hanging, with the combination in his hand, he unlocked the safe and drew out the bag containing the jewels. He had, however, been followed by some person unknown who struck him down and escaped with the gems.'

'The violent robbery, while shocking,' I noted, 'is nothing out of the ordinary. But this business of the painting, Holmes. Why on earth would the thief go to the bother of returning to the scene of the crime to substitute one painting in place of another?'

'It was perhaps a clue to his identity,' Pole suggested.

'That's not very likely,' Lestrade observed drily, 'unless he's Count Dracula – or Bela Lugosi.'

'Gentlemen,' said Holmes, quieting them with a gesture, 'your speculations, while amusing, perhaps, are not to the purpose. Now, Mr Bastable, let us marshal the facts and see where they lead us.'

'To Transylvania,' Pole suggested in a hushed aside to Lestrade.

Holmes ignored the facetious remark and fetched one of his pipes. 'Please describe the painting to us, Mr Bastable, and why you take it to be a portrait of the notorious vampire.'

'It was a dark-haired man with piercing eyes,' said Bastable, visibly paling at the memory, 'holding a cloak across the lower part of his face. Just as Mr Lugosi did in his portrayal of Dracula, concealing his fangs beneath the cover of his cloak as he advances on his victim.' By way of illustration he swung his forearm over his mouth and made his eyes bulge dramatically.

'Did your uncle Randolph have a taste for such gruesome decoration?' asked Holmes.

'Not at all, Mr Holmes,' said Bastable. 'When my uncle's lawyer was acquainting us with the contents of the will, he told us that Uncle Randolph was an avid collector of paintings by members of the so-called New English Art Club as well as works by those who are described as being of the New Venetian school, such as Henry Woods and John Singer Sargent.'

'In which case,' said Holmes, 'a portrait of the celebrated actor or of the notorious count himself would be out of place, to say the least.'

'Is this portrait of evil now to be found somewhere else in the house?' I wondered.

'A thorough search has been made,' Pole reported, 'and no painting resembling that just described has been uncovered.'

'And is there anywhere an empty space where the portrait of the girl might have originally hung?' asked Holmes, filling his pipe with tobacco.

'There is nothing to mark anywhere that picture might have been before being substituted for the macabre original,' Pole stated confidently. 'There are no empty spaces on any of the walls of the house.'

Holmes struck a match and lit his pipe, then took a long draw before speaking again. 'I take it, Mr Bastable, that when you saw the film *Dracula* it made a strong impression on you?'

'Yes. It was some years ago,' said Bastable, 'but I recall being unsettled by it to the extent that for several nights following I dreamed that I was being menaced by Lugosi in his role as the vampire.'

Holmes's gaze appeared to fix upon some far-off point in space while he continued to smoke. Lestrade and I were accustomed to his meditative silences, but after a few minutes, Bastable and Pole exchanged concerned glances.

'Perhaps, Mr Holmes,' said the country policeman, rising from his seat, 'we should leave you to your cogitation. Evidently this is an incident so outlandish that it taxes even your famed abilities.'

'Not at all,' said Holmes, waving at him to be seated. 'The matter is actually quite simple.'

Seeing that he had our full attention, he forced us to wait while he took three long puffs on his pipe before continuing.

'It is a well-known phenomenon of the human mind that it seeks patterns and connections even, or perhaps especially, when there are none. For example, when we see a face in the burning coals of a fireplace, or discern in the clouds the shape of a ship or a swan. Similarly, we might glimpse in passing something unknown to us and, when recollecting it, connect it to something familiar from our past experience.'

I confess that I did not yet see where Holmes's reasoning was leading, but I was sure he would soon come to the point, if only to dash Pole's galling assertion that the problem was beyond him.

'This is exactly the case with Mr Bastable's perception of the painting he thought he glimpsed as he hastened to his uncle's assistance,' Holmes continued. 'There exists a gulf of difference between what he caught out of the corner of his eye and what was really there.'

'Are you suggesting that there was no painting of Dracula,' said Bastable, somewhat miffed at being doubted, 'or of some equally sinister figure?'

'I am saying,' said Holmes, removing the pipe from his mouth and pointing the stem at the witness, 'that there was no painting at all.'

'Mr Holmes,' said Pole with a patronising chortle, 'if you are suggesting that there was only a blank wall, then you are quite wrong. As I have already explained, the oval area on the wall clearly proves that there was a painting of that shape hanging there before the substitution.'

'Yes, Mr Holmes, you cannot tell me that I simply imagined it,' Bastable asserted.

'Mr Bastable,' Holmes explained patiently, 'you and everyone else have been misled by the assumption that when you arrived on the scene your uncle's assailant was already gone.'

I had enough experience of Holmes's reasoning to see his point. 'Holmes, what you mean is that the robber was hiding in the alcove,' I guessed.

The approving twinkle in Holmes's eye was sufficient confirmation.

Both Pole and Bastable now appeared befuddled, and the policeman was frowning as though he feared some trick was being played on him.

'What happened was this,' said Holmes. 'Some member of the family had a suspicion that the letter Uncle Junius was keeping so confidential might well contain information of great value to whoever possessed it. Consequently, rather than go to bed, he kept up a late vigil and observed Junius Bastable creeping from his room and making his way stealthily down the stairs. Keeping back out of sight, he observed Junius pulling aside the hanging and opening the safe. As he crept closer he saw the older man making delighted examination of the jewels before he struck him down from behind. Why should our robber share this prize with the rest of the family when he could have it all for himself?

'He had only just snatched up the jewels when he heard you call out, Mr Bastable. He certainly could not afford to be caught in the act, so he dived into the alcove and pressed himself against the wall, out of your sight as you hurried down the short passage. While you were bent over the stricken victim, he sneaked back to his own rooms and concealed his prize. When you raised the alarm, he came rushing downstairs as though he had been asleep and pretended to be just as shocked as everyone else at what had taken place.'

'But, Mr Holmes,' said Pole with a shake of his head, 'this explains nothing about the painting.'

'Doesn't it?' said Holmes, genuinely surprised at his obtuseness. 'Surely it's clear enough that what Mr Bastable glimpsed was not a painting at all. It was a mirror.'

'A mirror?' gasped Bastable.

Pole appeared to have been struck speechless, while Lestrade slapped his knee to demonstrate his satisfaction with Holmes's insight.

'Imagine the thief's horror when he pressed himself into the alcove,' said Holmes, 'only to see – too late – that he stood exposed in the mirror facing him. In a moment of panic he threw his arm across his face, perhaps even yanking up the edge of his dressing gown, in a desperate effort to conceal his features. The piercing gaze you spoke of, Mr Bastable, was a result of his eyes growing wide in alarm.

'He realised at once the danger that Mr Bastable had spotted his reflection, even without its registering on his conscious mind. When, however, he noticed the mirror, he might then wonder, perhaps even guess, whose reflection he had caught a glimpse of. So, even as the alarm was being sounded, our robber snatched a painting from the wall of his own bedroom, hurried down to the alcove and swapped it for the mirror. The mirror itself he thrust into the nearest place of concealment until such time as he could remove it.'

Leaning forward intently, I asked my friend, 'So, Holmes, where is the mirror now?'

'Why, isn't that obvious? It now hangs in the place where the portrait of the girl with the rose originally hung, in order to conceal the fact that a picture had been removed, which would otherwise be clear from the residual outline.'

Bastable appeared to be pondering. 'Now that you've explained it, Mr Holmes, I now see a resemblance to my cousin James – the dark hair, the pale complexion.'

'I am confident, Mr Bastable, that if you and Detective Sergeant Pole examine your cousin James's room, you will find an oval mirror that does not match the outline behind it. The painting of the girl with the rose, on the other hand, will fit perfectly. The chances are very good that cousin James's fingerprints will be found on both, which will provide you with enough pressure to force him to surrender the stolen jewels.'

'Well, Mr Holmes,' said Pole, beaming as he rose, 'you are everything George Lestrade has told me. Maybe even cleverer.'

Bastable and Lestrade stood also.

'Yes, thank you ever so much, Mr Holmes,' said Bastable. 'Now that you have exposed the criminal for us, we can only hope and pray that my uncle makes a full recovery.'

'I'm sure we're all hoping for that,' I said, as Holmes and I accompanied our visitors to the door.

'You'd best hurry back to The Poplars, Oliver,' said Lestrade, 'before that thief takes it into his head to flee with the loot.'

'No fear of that, George,' Pole asserted confidently. 'I've put a guard on the house and nobody has been allowed to enter or leave.'

As Bastable and the country policeman made their way downstairs, Lestrade lingered in the doorway, edgily fingering his bowler hat.

'Is there something else, Lestrade?' I prompted.

'If I am not mistaken, this matter of the transformed painting merely served as an excuse for the inspector to call on us for the sake of some more important business,' Holmes surmised.

'You have the right of it there, Mr Holmes,' Lestrade conceded. He closed the door and came back into the room with an expression of heavy concern furrowing his large brow. 'I have a much more disturbing matter on my hands.'

3

THE INNER SANCTUM

Lestrade fumbled with his hat a few times more, then, shrugging off his obvious embarrassment, he set it down on the table. 'It's not strictly speaking a crime – more of a phenomenon, as they say. But I was wondering, Mr Holmes, if you might have any insight into this outbreak of spontaneous whadjamacallits.'

'Spontaneous human combustion,' I supplied.

Lestrade reacted with some relief. 'That's the thing, doctor. You've read about the cases, I suppose.'

'Only the newspaper accounts,' said Holmes, 'but as you say, it is difficult to classify them as crimes.'

'That's as may be,' said Lestrade, 'but there's been three of them in the past few weeks, and now *this* has got the commissioner breathing down my neck.'

Reaching into his pocket he pulled out a crumpled pamphlet which he handed to my friend. 'These have been produced by a woman evangelist who calls herself Miss Ophelia Faith and they're being spread about all over town.'

Holmes cast a cursory eye over the pamphlet and passed it to me. The cover proclaimed in large red letters THE DAY OF JUDGEMENT HAS ARRIVED!

Flipping it open, I read aloud from the first page. '*The evidence is before our eyes. Sinners are annihilated on our streets by an avenging fire. Men whose business is death have met their due punishment as a warning to the many. If you will not be washed in the Blood of the Lamb, you will be consumed by the Devil's Blaze.*'

There followed a series of fiery quotations from the Bible interspersed with further grim warnings.

'The victims of this phenomenon were, I believe, an army major, an official in the Home Office and a government scientist,' my friend recalled.

'That's correct, Mr Holmes,' Lestrade confirmed. 'Now I couldn't say whether there was anything specially sinful about any of them, but it strikes me as queer that they should all be part of the government establishment, so to speak.'

'One would not expect any purely natural phenomenon, however bizarre, to be quite so selective,' Holmes agreed.

'Added to which,' I said, handing the pamphlet back to Lestrade, 'if this phenomenon exists at all, which some would dispute, it is extremely rare. Three cases in the space of a few weeks, and all of them here in London, well, it is unprecedented.'

'Is Scotland Yard now pursuing this as a criminal investigation?' Holmes inquired.

Lestrade rubbed his jaw and shook his head unhappily. 'What the commissioner wants me to do is have a stern word with this Miss Ophelia Faith and warn her to stop stirring up a panic with her holy claptrap.'

'You would think the people of London have faced enough terrors,' I commented, 'between the Blitz and Crimson Jack's murders.'

'I just wondered, Mr Holmes,' Lestrade continued, visibly abashed, 'whether you've been looking into these combustions, you know, as a man who has a taste for the unusual, we might say.'

'I am not in the habit of chasing after the startling and the grotesque,' said Holmes, with an irked twitch of the mouth. 'I leave it to others to break up séances and disprove the existence of ghosts and monsters. In the case of these admittedly extraordinary incinerations, no one has engaged me to investigate them.'

'Until now perhaps,' I suggested. I had just heard Mrs Hudson answer the door and now she was dashing up the stairs with some urgency.

Holmes greeted my speculation with a raised eyebrow and a slow nod. A moment later, with scarcely a pause for the briefest of knocks, Mrs Hudson almost toppled into the room.

'A message for you, Mr Holmes,' she declared breathlessly. 'The gentleman downstairs said it is from the government and concerns the safety of the nation.'

She handed over an envelope, fingers trembling with excitement.

'I see from the stationery that it is indeed from Whitehall,' Holmes observed.

'It is from your brother, I take it,' I assumed.

'Not at all,' said Holmes unexpectedly. 'Mycroft is currently aboard the *Queen Mary* on his way to the United States.'

'Surely you're joking!' I exclaimed.

It was well known to me that Mycroft Holmes, who held one of the highest offices in the land, regarded even a short cab ride as an insufferable inconvenience and had only agreed to establish himself in a Whitehall office because a German bomb had rendered his beloved Diogenes Club uninhabitable. I could not imagine any force that might compel him to endure the rigours of an ocean voyage.

'He is accompanying the prime minister on a visit to our allies,' Holmes informed me. 'Mr Churchill was most insistent, and when Mohammed commands, even the mountain must move.'

He plucked from his desk the small throwing dagger he kept as a souvenir of our confrontation with the Black Lotus Tong, and used it to slice open the envelope. Pulling a single sheet from within, he took only a moment to scan the contents.

'We are honoured indeed, Watson. We have been invited – if one may use so polite a word – to a meeting of the Intelligence Inner Council.' With a glance at the inspector he added, 'I assume, Lestrade, that they share the same concern as your commissioner. Let us hope that Miss Ophelia Faith is mistaken in her attribution and that we will not find ourselves in direct conflict with Lucifer.'

The next morning, as we walked up the Mall towards our appointment, I noted an energy in Holmes's stride that I had not seen in some weeks, a sure sign that the affair of the devil's blaze had fully engaged his interest. I myself felt equally invigorated by the sunshine streaming down from a peaceful sky and the musical piping of the robins and sparrows in the trees of St James's Park. A bright red bus rumbled by with an advertisement for liver salts pasted along its side, while all around the bustle of Londoners about their everyday business created an atmosphere of such normality it was almost possible to forget the dreadful struggle in which we were all engaged in our own particular ways.

Ahead, the sweeping curve of Admiralty Arch with its three majestic archways impressed me as much as ever, even more so as I was aware that much of our war effort was being directed from this distinctive edifice. While its upper floors were occupied by numerous military and intelligence personnel, much of the most vital work was being carried out in the maze of tunnels beneath street level. Though Mycroft Holmes was not a member of the Intelligence Inner Council, who held their meetings here, they frequently consulted him on matters of national importance. It seemed that in his absence they were compelled to turn to the only man who could match him in intellect and ingenuity, his brother Sherlock Holmes.

Once we had presented ourselves at the entrance, we were escorted upstairs, our identities being checked at three separate points before we were finally admitted to the inner sanctum. In a spacious, well-lighted chamber dominated by a full length portrait of the Duke of Wellington, seven distinguished men sat round a large table with notepads and bulging folders set out before them. They rose as one to greet us with differing degrees of enthusiasm.

One or two I recognised while others, I was aware, occupied such sensitive positions that their names were covered in a shroud of impenetrable secrecy. Sir Anthony Lloyd, in his dark suit and Oxford tie, was the head of the council. Beneath his habitual air of reserved formality, I could tell he was relieved to see us as he shook hands.

'Mr Holmes, I am very glad you are available to meet with us. You too, Dr Watson. Really, Holmes, your brother Mycroft has chosen a most inconvenient time to be absent.'

'Yes, he no sooner departs for America,' Holmes observed, 'than prominent people begin bursting into flame.'

Sir Anthony was impressed in spite of himself. 'So you've guessed why we called you here.'

'It hardly requires guesswork,' said Holmes. 'Given the resources at your command, only the most extraordinary events would compel you to call upon the services of a mere detective.'

'I still don't see that it is necessary.' The comment came from Admiral Sir John Prentiss, who, in full naval uniform, stood by a wall map of Europe, as though contemplating some grand strategy. He thrust his hands unhappily into his pockets. 'This is hardly a matter for civilians.'

'I trust then, Sir John, that you have a military solution to propose,' I countered. My friend treated me to a thin smile as I came to his defence.

The admiral let out a loud harumph and hunched his shoulders defiantly.

'In the absence of Mr Mycroft Holmes,' said the suave Captain Roland Shore, who in spite of his military rank was dressed in a grey suit and wing collar, 'I think we should welcome whatever insights his brother might have to offer.' He tapped his cigarette on the edge of an ashtray as though dismissing the admiral's objections along with the excess ash.

Holmes took up position in front of the ornate marble fireplace and folded his arms as he cast his gaze over the assembled dignitaries. 'I take it, gentlemen, that there is a consensus among you that this is no natural phenomenon?'

'Quite so, Holmes,' said Colonel Jerome Lawford, whose broad shoulders impressively filled out his army uniform. 'The first might be taken as such, perhaps even a second, but three . . .' He shook his head and his bushy moustache seemed to curl in displeasure.

'And all of them men of importance,' Sir Anthony Lloyd concluded, drumming his fingers on the casing of a large radio set. 'I greatly fear that we are faced with a new form of attack by a desperate and ruthless enemy.'

'Desperate?' I echoed. 'To hear the pronouncements of Herr Goebbels, one would imagine that Germany and her allies are on the brink of victory.'

'Oh, even with the Americans on board,' said Roland Shore, 'there's still a hard slog ahead.'

'But we've pretty much mopped up what's left of Rommel's army in North Africa,' Lawford reported with satisfaction, 'and we're already making plans for a landing in Sicily.'

'According to our sources,' said Sir Anthony, 'Mussolini may soon be deposed and Italy withdraw from its alliance with the Nazis.'

'And then there is Russia,' said Admiral Prentiss with a gloomy glance at the map. 'Hitler and Stalin are engaged in a series of savage battles which may decide the entire future course of the war.'

'I think we are all aware,' said Sir Anthony, 'that the enemy we face is far from defeated and even now plans a counterstrike. We know for a fact that they are developing a self-propelled bomb which they aim to deploy within a matter of months. It is not beyond them to produce other terror weapons as well.'

'Such as a new form of incendiary,' said Holmes.

'What other explanation can there be?' said Captain Shore.

'We have to assume,' said Sir Anthony, 'that German agents have smuggled such a device into the country and are testing it on a small scale before launching a more devastating attack.'

'You say *assume*, Sir Anthony,' said Holmes. 'Do you have any evidence?'

'As yet we have found no connection to any human agency,' said Shore. 'This fire seems to strike like lightning. If it was more random in its targets, we might shrug it off, but the victims – Major General Talman, Sir Leopold Denby, Dr Wallace Carew – such men have surely been specifically singled out for assassination.'

'Talman was incinerated during a staff meeting with some of his junior officers,' said Colonel Lawford.

'Sir Leopold burst into flames while at home with his wife,' added Lloyd, 'and Carew was consumed by fire in the middle of the street before a score of horrified witnesses.'

It was at that moment, almost as if conjured up by his words, that the horror revealed itself in our very midst.

4

THE GHOST OF EVIL

I noticed that Captain Roland Shore had stubbed out his cigarette and was tugging agitatedly at his shirt collar.

'I say,' he grunted, 'it's getting damnably hot in here.'

As he appeared to be suffering some distress, I took a step forward, intending to offer my medical assistance. I froze in my tracks as a piercing cry broke from his lips, causing everyone in the room to turn towards him.

There was a communal gasp of horror as flames erupted beneath his clothing and burned right through his shirt front. He screamed and staggered as the fire raced up and down his body, melting his features and igniting his hair.

'Watson, the curtains!'

The commanding voice of Sherlock Holmes shook me from my horrified stupor and propelled me into action. Together we ripped a heavy curtain from the nearest window and made a rush for Shore. An agonised shriek was choked off in his throat as he swayed from side to side in the midst of the inferno. He crumpled to the floor even as we flung the curtain about him to smother the flames.

Holmes and I held the covering down tightly, our nostrils assailed by the acrid stench of charred flesh. We felt a final spasm as the fire died at last.

Holmes stood up and watched as I partially unwrapped the body and felt at what was left of the man's throat for any trace of life. With a sad shake of the head I rose. 'Most likely he died from shock rather than the ravages of the fire,' I said.

The members of the council stood pale and shaken, doubly so as they had long regarded themselves as guarded from any attack by layers of heavy security.

'My God!' Sir Anthony Lloyd gasped. 'This is impossible!'

'How?' exclaimed Admiral Prentiss, taking a step towards the dead man then turning away abruptly. 'How could they strike at us here?'

Colonel Lawford straightened his shoulders defiantly. 'Gentlemen,' he stated gruffly, 'it appears nowhere is safe from this menace. Nowhere on Earth.'

These were men who had witnessed their share of horrors but every face in the room was blanched of colour. I had seen men die grotesquely from poisoned gas on the battlefield, but Shore's death, striking as it did out of the blue with terrifying suddenness, was the most dreadful spectacle I had ever beheld.

Two armed soldiers came crashing through the door, belatedly drawn by Captain Shore's screams. Lloyd brought them up short with an upraised hand.

'I'm sorry, there's nothing you can do,' he informed them solemnly. 'Send for a van to take Captain Shore's body to the mortuary. We'll need to arrange an examination.'

The soldiers gaped at the smouldering remains, both of them rendered speechless by the awful spectacle.

'Mr Holmes,' said Lloyd, struggling to regain his composure, 'it seems the matter is even more urgent than we thought. The council itself is now the target of this unseen enemy.'

'I swear to you, Sir Anthony, that I shall get to the bottom of this,' Holmes promised. His grim resolve was evident in the firm set of his mouth and the hard glint in his hawk-like eyes.

The atmosphere at Baker Street had rarely been so electric. Witnessing that horrid death with his own eyes had galvanised Sherlock Holmes to a level of intense concentration I had rarely beheld in our long association. We were surrounded by police files, coroners' reports and newspapers, but as far as I could tell none of them shed any light upon the dreadful deaths. It was as though the smoke from those fires blinded us so that we were groping about in the dark.

'I confess myself at a loss,' I declared, closing the last page on a sheaf of notes. 'The coroner in each case was completely baffled and there is nothing in the medical history of any of these men to indicate the preconditions for such a grisly demise.'

'And while all the victims played prominent roles in public life,' said Holmes, tossing aside a loose-leafed folder, 'I can find no direct connection between them. They are certainly members of the military, scientific and political institutions, but not so prominent that they should be specially singled out for assassination.'

'You believe that these are assassinations then, Holmes?' When he grunted his assent I proceeded. 'Then surely Sir Anthony is correct and this is the work of German agents based here in London.'

'If these German agents are able to strike from the shadows at any target they choose, why not go after bigger game?' Holmes demanded. 'Why not strike directly at Downing Street?'

'Perhaps the aim is to cause terror,' I surmised, 'by seeming to kill at random then work towards the highest in the land once the whole city is already in a panic.'

Holmes grimaced. 'Given the example of the Blitz, I would not expect our enemies to be so subtle in their methods. There are age-old tales of men bursting into flame, but we must free ourselves from the shackles of myth if we are to find our way to the truth.'

'Might it be possible,' I suggested hesitantly, 'that what we are dealing with is not spontaneous human combustion but something even more strange?'

Holmes paused in filling his pipe. 'Whatever do you mean, Watson?'

'Have you ever heard of the phenomenon of pyrokinesis – the ability to generate and control fire by the power of the mind?'

Holmes scoffed. 'Yes, I have heard of it and dismissed it as arrant nonsense.'

'You might do well to reconsider,' I persisted doggedly. 'If this is not a bizarre phenomenon of nature but the result of some human agency, how then is it being so directed that it can penetrate the walls of one of the most secure buildings in the country?'

'How indeed?' Holmes scowled and tapped the stem of his pipe against his chin. 'Surely there is some fiendish ingenuity at work here.'

'Fiendish is right,' I agreed. 'To kill a man is one thing, but to choose to do so by incinerating him – well, it might as well be the work of the devil.'

Holmes lit his pipe and took several slow draws, as though pondering a new and disturbing thought. When he spoke again his tone was sombre.

'For some years now I have been aware of an intelligence operating unseen, orchestrating a series of apparently unrelated events – robberies, embezzlements, kidnappings – all of which form part of an elaborate web of crime.'

I was surprised he had never mentioned this notion of his before. 'Intelligence? You mean some sort of espionage organisation?'

Holmes bit down on his pipe and shook his head. 'No, I speak of one man – one ruthless, determined man whose intellect may well be the equal of my own.'

'The equal of yours, Holmes? Surely not!' My shock at the possibility of so dangerous a rival was matched by my surprise that Holmes should acknowledge any adversary as his equal.

'It is true, Watson. There exists out there, unknown to the public, a mind as brilliant and highly trained as my own, dedicated not to justice but to crime, merciless crime on a vast and ruinous scale.'

'You think this unnamed mastermind may be behind the fiery terror?'

'It is possible. If any man alive is capable of perpetrating such horrors, it is he, though I am at a loss in this instance to divine his purpose.'

'But, Holmes, who is this man and why have you not spoken to me of him before?'

'My dear friend,' Holmes responded grimly, 'he has such power at his fingertips that even to breathe his name in the wrong context is to invite assassination. I would not lay you under that shadow, not unless it becomes a matter of the most pressing necessity.'

'Surely, though, you have been making moves to thwart him?' I exclaimed.

Holmes sprang from his chair and paced the room like a restless tiger in an effort to work off his frustration.

'I had him under observation for some time and was gathering a growing collection of evidence that proved his complicity in these crimes. I followed a thin thread of clues through the labyrinth to the centre where the monster himself dwells unseen and enjoys the fruits of his schemes out of sight and out of reach of the law. However, with the outbreak of war, he disappeared, closeting himself in some secret refuge where none of my sources or operatives could track him.'

'He has fled abroad, surely, feeling your breath hot on his neck.'

Holmes ceased his pacing and rested an elbow against the mantelpiece. 'No, Watson. For among the many crimes that continue to plague our country, even in time of war, there are those rare few that continue to bear his signature, turning as they do on some ingenious contrivance well beyond the imagination of any ordinary villain. Mark my words, he is still out there, but somehow he has found the means to elude me before I could close my trap upon him.'

'Are you saying then that he has added invisibility to his other attributes?' I blurted.

A mirthless smile touched Holmes's lips. 'As good as.

It is as though his very existence has been obliterated, and yet he still works his mischief like a ghost.'

I felt a chill come over me to think that anyone might bend a genius as great as Holmes's to the ends of evil and at the same time put himself beyond the reach of justice. Silence lay heavy upon the room, so much so that I was relieved when Mrs Hudson appeared at the door with a note that had just been delivered.

Once she had scurried back downstairs Holmes opened the envelope and withdrew a small handwritten note.

'It's from Sir Anthony Lloyd,' he said, passing me the paper. It read, *Please go at once to the Ramsay Building on Gower Place to consult with our expert. A.L.*

'Expert?' I repeated. 'Expert in what, I wonder. The paranormal?'

'Hardly that, Watson,' said Holmes with only a hint of mockery. 'The Ramsay Building houses the chemistry department of University College London.'

5

AN UNEXPECTED REUNION

The porter at the door of the Ramsay Building was a stout fellow in a faded uniform and peaked cap. He was clearly expecting us and greeted us warmly.

'So this is the great Sherlock Holmes, eh? To be honest with you, sir, I might not have recognised you without the funny hat.'

Holmes quirked an irritable eyebrow. 'Funny hat?'

'Yes, sir,' the porter responded affably. 'You know, the one with the flaps,' he expanded, miming the act of pulling them down over his ears.

'Holmes, I believe he means the deerstalker,' I explained helpfully.

'Thank you, Watson,' Holmes snapped. 'I know perfectly well what he means.' His voice rose to an aggrieved pitch. 'I am photographed once – *once*, I say – while trekking across Dartmoor in an Inverness cape and deerstalker, a costume entirely suited to the landscape. That picture is then reprinted innumerable times in every newspaper until it is emblazoned upon the popular imagination to the point where it is assumed to be the only headgear in my wardrobe. I would no more be seen wearing such a hat on the streets of London than I would attend the opera in an Apache war bonnet and Wellington boots.'

'Of course, sir, of course,' said the porter, turning away hurriedly to lead us inside. 'No offence intended, I'm sure.'

We were escorted down a long corridor to a heavy fire door, which the porter heaved open for us before returning to his post. As we entered the spacious laboratory we were immediately aware of the hiss of gas and the gurgle of boiling liquids. I caught a whiff of carbolic acid as well as other less familiar odours. An assortment of sinks and cabinets was arrayed along the left-hand wall and a series of long wooden tables ran the length of the room, all of them covered with test tubes, jars of chemicals, Bunsen burners and other scientific paraphernalia. At the far end of the room a white-coated figure wearing goggles was hunched over a work bench. At the sound of the door creaking shut, the scientist looked up.

'Ah, Mr Holmes and Dr Watson,' said a familiar voice with a pronounced Scottish accent. 'I've been waiting for you to show up.'

As we drew closer she removed her goggles and I recognised her face at once. 'Why, Holmes, it's Dr MacReady!' I exclaimed.

We had encountered Dr Elspeth MacReady the previous year at a research installation in the Scottish Highlands. As she was an expert in petrochemicals and accelerants, I supposed she had been reassigned here on account of the recent spate of incendiary deaths.

'Dr MacReady – this is an unexpected pleasure,' said Holmes with an approving nod.

I was surprised by the warmth of my friend's greeting. While unfailingly courteous to members of the opposite sex, he was generally both formal and reserved in his dealings with them.

'We do seem to meet only in the most unusual circumstances,' said the doctor.

'You are certainly a long way from Castle Dunfillan,' I observed.

'Och, my work in that place is all done. For the past few months I've been in Portsmouth helping the Navy to develop new sealants for submarine repair. Then the word came that some intelligence chappies want me to look into this outbreak of fiery deaths.'

She gestured towards some beakers and test tubes, the contents of which were bubbling over the flames of Bunsen burners. I noted also samples of ash and other substances, gathered, so I supposed, from the remains of the victims.

'You are familiar then with the phenomenon of spontaneous human combustion?' Holmes inquired.

'Oh aye. A year or two ago I published an article about it in the *Journal of Pyrotic Studies*. But I'm not the only one to take an interest. Coroner Gavin Thurston made his own assessment in the *British Medical Journal* back in 1938.'

Holmes was examining a cat's cradle of an arrangement of glass pipes on a nearby work bench. 'And yet it has a longer history than that,' he said.

'You're right there,' Dr MacReady agreed. 'The first use of the term goes back to 1746 when Paul Rolli used it in the journal *Philosophical Transactions* to refer to the mysterious death of Countess Cornelia Zangheri Bandi.'

She picked up a test tube, gave it a shake and squinted at its murky contents before placing it back on its rack. 'There were quite a few cases recorded after that until it was so well established that Dickens used it to cause the death of Mr Krook in his novel *Bleak House*. He put a lot of research in while writing his story.'

My interest as a medical man was understandably piqued. 'And have your own researches led to any conclusions?'

'Well, I'll not buy the notion, put about by some, of fire generating spontaneously inside the human body,' the Scotswoman answered, 'though, to be sure, the body does contain plenty of fat that will burn like candle wax, as well as a good deal of hydrogen and methane.'

As she spoke, she used a pair of tongs to remove a beaker of brown liquid from the flame which had been heating it.

'Is this an experiment to determine the cause, then?' I wondered, pointing to the beaker.

'No, Dr Watson,' she answered, pouring the liquid into a tin cup, 'this is my morning coffee. Would you care for a wee drop?'

I declined, and noticed that Holmes was strolling around the laboratory, staring with deep interest at the advanced equipment. He took a quick glance at the contents of an industrial refrigeration unit, then asked, 'How then to account for the many recorded cases?'

'Some of them have a lot of features in common,' said Dr MacReady, taking a sip of black coffee. 'To begin with, there's a high incidence of alcoholism among the victims, especially in the records from Victorian times when folk of low character were expected to come to a sticky end. In spite of my strict Presbyterian upbringing, though, I don't think enjoying a few nips leads directly to a punishing dose of hellfire.'

'The coincidence is suggestive, however,' I commented.

'It is,' said Dr MacReady. 'The fact is that most of the victims were incapacitated by ill health, obesity or inebriation. This being so, there's every likelihood that should they catch fire, for whatever reason, they wouldn't be able to save themselves. Then there will be cases where the victim has died of a heart attack or stroke and was set on fire subsequently.'

'And the source of the fire?' inquired Holmes, scrutinising the labels on a shelf of chemicals. 'There is supposedly some mystery surrounding that.'

'In most cases,' said Dr MacReady, 'there was certainly an external source – a candle, a lamp, a fireplace and, of course, the notorious dropped cigarette. Mind, though, that the folk telling these stories often left that information out.'

'Yes, persons will very often omit certain facts in order to make a good yarn,' said Holmes with a sardonic smile. 'Don't you agree, Watson?'

'I have known such cases,' I conceded, refusing to accept this slight on my own literary efforts. 'But surely the extent of some of these combustions is beyond the relatively minor sources you have listed.'

'All that's needed, doctor,' the Scotswoman explained, 'is a flammable garment or a cotton wrap to provide fuel. But even without that, a cigarette could char the victim's clothing badly enough to break the skin and so release the subcutaneous fat. Once that's absorbed into the material it makes a very effective wick.'

'What we witnessed,' said Holmes, 'was a man – fit and healthy, to all appearances – bursting into flame as suddenly as you would flick on a light switch, not some drunkard stumbling into a fireplace.'

'Was there a possible source of ignition?' Dr MacReady inquired.

'He was smoking a cigarette,' I recalled. 'He put it out just as his queer turn came on.'

'I don't believe that cigarette had any role in the tragedy,' Holmes stated.

'You're right there,' Dr MacReady agreed. 'Four of these incidents following on that close to one another – no, they can't be accidents.'

'Which leaves us with what?' I wondered.

Dr MacReady swallowed the last of her coffee and set the tin cup down with a clatter. 'The possibility that they were exposed to some agent that, when activated, reacts with the chemicals in the body to produce a fire.'

'How close are you then to cornering this agent?' Holmes inquired, casting an approving eye over the array of chemical equipment.

Dr MacReady's lips tightened. 'Not close at all. You'll know yourself, Mr Holmes, it's a slow enough process testing for something you expect. But searching for something unknown is a proper trauchle. There's no telling how long it might take.'

'At least we are assured that the matter is in the very best of hands,' said Holmes.

Dr MacReady cocked her head. 'You flatter me, Mr Holmes. I know that you're no mean chemist yourself.'

'True,' Holmes agreed without modesty. 'But I believe my talents will be put to best use tracking down whoever is behind these terrible attacks before they strike again.'

As we walked to the doorway, Dr MacReady called after us, 'Mr Holmes, you be sure to be careful. There's a dangerous beast at large somewhere out there.'

'I shall take every precaution,' Holmes assured her as we exited the laboratory.

Little did I suspect then that we were about to encounter a fresh danger that was entirely unforeseen.

6

HUNTERSWOOD

When the phone rang next morning Holmes was fully engaged in playing Paganini's Cantabile in D upon his Stradivarius. I laid down my paper and picked up the receiver.

'Hello. Dr Watson speaking.'

'Ah, Watson, Lloyd here. There is a car downstairs waiting to take you and Mr Holmes to Hunterswood. There is someone there I believe can be of great help to you in your investigation.'

'Might I ask who that is?'

'I'm afraid that for security reasons we can only refer to him as M.'

Irked by such foolishness, I could not refrain from commenting, 'Well, I hope the alphabet contains sufficient letters to encompass all your security needs.'

With absolute seriousness he said, 'We also have numbers,' and then hung up.

'So, Watson,' said Holmes, setting his instrument aside, 'a car is waiting for us outside.'

'Surely your hearing cannot be so acute as that,' I protested.

'No, but as you were speaking I saw your eyes dart at the window. It was Sir Anthony Lloyd, of course.'

'For goodness' sake, Holmes, how can you know it was he?'

'Thanks to your time in the military, old friend, your posture always stiffens when you speak to someone in authority,' Holmes explained.

'I suppose you have also deduced where we are to be driven to?' I inquired pointedly.

Holmes raised an eyebrow. 'Really, Watson, I'm not a magician,' he chided.

'Very well then,' I said. 'We are to be taken to Hunterswood. I have heard of the place. I believe it is a convalescent home for officers suffering from physical and psychological trauma.'

'And what is the purpose of this journey?'

'We are to speak to someone there who it seems can be of help to us. Sir Anthony would only refer to him as M.'

Holmes scoffed. 'How these government functionaries love to cast a cloud of mystery over the most mundane matters.'

When we descended to the street a few minutes later we saw a pretty young woman in a WRNS uniform standing by a grey Hillman 10 saloon car. She greeted us with a perky smile as she opened the back door.

'Mr Holmes, Dr Watson, I'm Wren Jane Garrick. I've been assigned to drive you to Hunterswood.'

I noted that our driver had dark curls and a trim figure. 'I'm sure it will be a very pleasant ride,' I complimented her, as we climbed in.

As Jane Garrick got into the driver's seat, Holmes addressed her very casually. 'I suppose, Wren Garrick, that you are well acquainted with Hunterswood.'

'I'm sorry, but I'm afraid I'm not permitted to talk about it,' the young woman told us with polite finality.

Starting up the engine, she slid shut a glass partition that separated the driver from the passengers, so cutting off any further inquiries.

Holmes contemplated the back of the Wren's head as we moved off. 'I wonder why she is so tight-lipped about a convalescent home,' he said, 'and who it is Sir Anthony Lloyd wishes us to meet there.'

'Might it be, Holmes, that Hunterswood is home to a survivor of one of these incendiary attacks?' I suggested. 'If so, perhaps he has in his possession some clue as to who or what is behind them.'

Holmes tapped a knuckle thoughtfully against the window. 'That is a plausible speculation, Watson, given the limited information presented to us.'

Gratified that my suggestion appeared to have some merit, I felt encouraged to expand upon my thought. 'I hope,' I said, 'that the poor fellow has not been badly disfigured. I know there have been advances in corrective surgery, but this phenomenon is quite ruinous and the mental effects are likely to be extreme.'

Holmes's thoughts, however, were moving in a different direction. He suddenly interjected, 'Tell me, Watson, you move in some rather broad medical circles, don't you?'

'Yes,' I affirmed, puzzled that he should question something so obvious.

'In all your wide acquaintance,' he continued, 'have you ever come across anyone who has been treated at Hunterswood?'

I pondered for a moment. 'No, I can't say that I have.'

'And is there anyone among your colleagues who

has ever worked there? Do you know of anyone who is currently on the staff?'

Again I searched my memory before answering. 'No. As far as I am aware, very few of them have even heard of it.'

'Curious, isn't it?' Holmes stroked his chin thoughtfully. 'One might almost imagine that it isn't a medical facility at all.'

'What are you getting at, Holmes? If it isn't a convalescent home then what is it?'

'That we shall discover when we get there, along with the identity of an individual so important that our meeting with him is shrouded in veils of secrecy.'

We headed north-west out of London. Holmes passed most of the journey in a thoughtful silence while I contemplated the lovely countryside of Buckinghamshire rolling by. Reflecting back over my earlier speculation, it seemed unlikely that anyone could survive the sort of conflagration we had seen consume Captain Shore. But as we already had an expert chemist assisting us, who else could possibly bring a fresh light to bear on this baffling case?

As we passed through the pleasant village of Huntingford I saw a sign on the door of the old Norman church advertising a garden fête. On the green outside the Blacksmith's Arms public house a band of local worthies were enjoying a game of bowls with much cheering and laughter. Jane Garrick rolled down her window and waved to a pair of girls in civilian dress emerging from a busy sweet shop. They beamed as they waved back, from which I inferred that our pretty driver must be stationed here.

A couple of miles further on we reached the entrance to a large estate surrounded by a high stone wall that had been augmented with barbed wire. The castellated gatehouse was manned by armed soldiers who motioned us to stop. Jane Garrick showed them her papers and explained who her passengers were. The sentries took a few moments to scrutinise us before waving us on.

The carriageway took us past rows of elm and lime trees before opening out into a broad drive. We pulled up outside a large country house of red brick and black slate that seemed to combine several disparate architectural styles, as though deliberately flouting conventional tastes.

Our driver hopped out. As she moved to open the rear door for us, a motorbike rider roared up from the direction of the gate and growled to a halt only a few feet from her.

'Excuse me, miss,' he said, pushing up his goggles the better to appreciate the girl he was addressing. 'Can you tell me where to take coded naval dispatches?'

She smiled pleasantly and pointed. 'You want Hut Six, over there by that yew tree.'

'Ta very much,' said the messenger. He kicked his mount back into life and raced off.

Holmes and I emerged from the car without her aid and gazed about us with great interest. A number of long wooden huts surrounded the house, laid out apparently at random. A complex array of aerials rose from many of the huts as well as from the roof of the house. Certainly there was nothing to indicate a convalescent home: no men on crutches or being rolled about in wheelchairs; no sign of nurses or other medical attendants.

Jane Garrick beckoned us to the path that led up to the big house. As we followed, two men emerged from a nearby hut engaged in a most animated conversation. Holmes nodded in their direction.

'Do you see, Watson? That chap with the thatch of yellow hair is Weldon Tremaine, England's youngest ever chess grand master, and the bearded gentleman with whom he is conversing is Professor Sinclair Barraclough, the noted linguist who translated those passages of the lost Punic language preserved in the *Miles Gloriosus* of Plautus.'

'Really?' I said. 'What on earth can have brought them here?'

Holmes indicated another individual seated on a bench by the front door of the house, wearing a straw hat and utterly absorbed in scribbling in a large notepad.

'That fellow in the straw hat is surely Miles Rawson.'

'And who might he be?' I wondered. 'A famous composer, I suppose, or something equally distinguished.'

'In a manner of speaking he is a composer. He is the man who devises the *Times* crossword puzzle. You will recall last year's famous challenge nicknamed the Gordian Knot, which was created by Rawson. The prize for its completion was three hundred pounds, but it was so fiendishly difficult the money was never claimed.'

'So no one was able to solve it?' I stared at the man in the straw hat with a fresh measure of respect.

'No one except me, of course,' said Holmes airily. 'But I thought it would be vulgar to claim the reward.'

'Chess? Dead languages? Crossword puzzles? What on earth can have drawn such diverse characters to this place?'

'Watson, surely you see that their presence tells us the true purpose of Hunterswood.' Holmes spoke softly, with one eye on Wren Garrick ahead of us. 'This is an intelligence centre and these are exactly the sorts of men who would be recruited to crack the codes used by the enemy. It is entirely possible that this place is the key to winning the war.'

'I see. Hence the secrecy.'

'Yes, and the cover story that it is a convalescent home. I suppose we should feel privileged to be let in on the secret.'

Our driver ushered us through the front door into a spacious vestibule floored in gleaming black and white tiles. At the far end a stairway of polished oak ascended to the mezzanine. Through an open door to our right I could glimpse a ballroom from which issued the familiar strains of 'By a Pale Lagoon' and the scuffle of dancing feet. It sounded very incongruous in a place dedicated to high intellectual pursuits, but I was well aware of the importance of leisure activities in maintaining morale.

We were directed to a reception desk attended by a thin-faced woman in a bright floral blouse. After taking our names she made a brief call on her telephone. Setting down the receiver, she said, 'Jeremy is on his way to take you to the director's office.'

'I'll leave you now,' Jane Garrick told us. Turning to the receptionist, she said, 'When Mr Holmes and Dr Watson are ready to return to London, you'll know where to find me.'

'I certainly will,' said the thin lady, arching a pencilled eyebrow. She addressed us in hushed tones as our driver departed. 'She's been spending a lot of time with Captain Willis from Army Intelligence. The talk is all over the mess hall.'

Her prominent blue eyes were sparkling. She clearly relished the opportunity to impart some local gossip to outsiders who hadn't heard it before. Holmes took his usual observant interest in our surroundings and spotted a figure coming down the stairs towards us. It was a young man with smooth flaxen hair who peered at us through his pince-nez. This, I supposed, was Jeremy.

Pausing on the bottom step, he said, 'If you would follow me, please, gentlemen.'

Our destination proved to be a room on the second floor. It was furnished like the antechamber of a law office, with leather chairs, scattered side tables and an assortment of nondescript prints decorating the walls. Jeremy headed for a further door at the far end of the room and waved us towards the seating. 'Gentlemen, if you will wait here, Professor Moriarty will see you shortly.'

He disappeared into the inner office, closing the door quietly behind him.

'Moriarty, eh?' I said. 'I suppose that explains why they refer to him as M.'

I was about to sit down when I noticed that Holmes's frame had gone completely rigid and that his saturnine features were drained of colour. He had every appearance of a man who has just received a debilitating shock.

'Holmes, old man,' I inquired with deep concern, 'are you quite all right?'

He was slow to respond and turned to me with a glazed look, as though bestirring himself from a swoon. When he spoke, his voice was low and husky with a depth of emotion such as he only rarely displayed.

'Watson, that name – Moriarty – that is the man I was speaking of when I told you of that supreme and evil intelligence which had eluded me. We have, all unsuspecting, walked straight into his lair.'

7

A FATEFUL MEETING

I barely had time to absorb this chilling revelation before the young man – I assumed him to be M's secretary – reappeared.

'This way, if you please, gentlemen.'

He ushered us into the inner office and withdrew, closing the door behind him. I had an immediate impression of a room furnished in a modernist style with sharp angles and small, glass-topped tables, as I braced myself to confront the arch-genius of evil Holmes believed awaited us. At first glance, the man seated behind the desk, his fingers steepled before him, could hardly have appeared more harmless.

He was sleek and dapper like a successful bank manager and his hooded eyes regarded us with a disinterested languor. His slicked-back hair, however, displayed a large brow that suggested a wide-reaching intellect. He did not rise to greet us but merely nodded by way of acknowledgement.

The initial shock of discovering his enemy was waiting behind the door seemed to have braced Holmes like a dash of cold water. There was about him an air of steely composure, like that of a man committed to a stern test of strength.

'Professor Moriarty, may I say I have long anticipated this meeting.'

Moriarty's smile was without warmth. 'As have I, Mr Holmes. It has about it an air of fateful inevitability. Do please be seated.'

As we settled ourselves into a pair of white leather chairs, Jeremy returned with a sheaf of documents in his hand.

'What are those papers?' the professor demanded.

'Agreements to abide by the terms of the Official Secrets Act, of course,' explained Jeremy. 'Surely these guests of yours will have to sign them before we can allow them to leave Hunterswood.'

Moriarty tutted and waved him away. 'I hardly think that is necessary. I am sure we can trust Mr Holmes and Dr Watson to be absolutely discreet.'

Once his secretary had left, Moriarty made an open-handed gesture. 'After all, Mr Holmes, the government itself is your client and you are bound therefore by your own code of confidentiality.'

'Quite so, professor,' Holmes responded drily. 'It is gratifying to find you so well versed in matters of professional ethics.'

'I find it instructive to observe how much the lives of others are constricted by rules and regulations.'

Since Moriarty appeared disposed to ignore me, I took a moment to survey the room. I was struck – not to say repulsed – by the paintings which decked the walls. They were all products of the most modern schools, meaning that some consisted of clashing geometric patterns while others presented grotesque distortions of the human form. They contributed in no small measure to the unwelcoming iciness of the atmosphere.

The paintings had also drawn Holmes's attention. 'I see, professor, you have some of the more abstract works of Wadsworth and Pasmore,' he observed. 'You have even got your hands on a Mondrian. Such works of art are surely rather an expensive taste for one on an academic's salary.'

Moriarty allowed himself a guarded smirk. 'You'd be surprised at some of the perks my current position affords me.'

'Far more than your previous post, I'm sure,' said Holmes. 'Your college is under the impression that you are on an extended sabbatical at the University of British Columbia.'

Moriarty picked up a silver fountain pen from his desk and tapped it against the palm of his hand. 'You will appreciate, Mr Holmes, that my work here must remain absolutely confidential, even at the cost of a few innocent falsehoods.'

'So we are correct in believing this to be an intelligence gathering centre,' I interposed.

Moriarty's eyes flickered briefly in my direction, as though he were only now becoming aware of my presence. 'Indeed, doctor. You will have observed that we have our own arrays of radio receivers, in addition to which intelligence reports and intercepts are brought to me here from every part of the world.'

'Dealing with such an influx of information must be quite a strain upon your resources,' Holmes remarked.

'We have almost nine thousand men and women working here,' the professor informed us, 'most of whom are engaged in breaking enemy codes. Every message deciphered could mean lives saved here or ships sunk there.'

Holmes leaned forward only slightly, but it was enough to give him the appearance of a hawk descending on its prey. 'I'm surprised that such responsibilities leave you time to direct that other business of yours which is shrouded in an even greater obscurity than your official work here at Hunterswood.'

Moriarty leaned back in his chair and spread his palms out before him in a gesture of blamelessness worthy of Pontius Pilate. 'I'm sure I have no idea what you're talking about.'

'To take only a few instances, there was the blackmailing of Lord Asterbury, which led directly to his suicide; the disappearance of the freighter *Arctic Star*; the Peruvian silver mine scandal; the tragic events in the Welsh village of Tragethin. Need I go on?'

It seemed to me that, having now come face to face with the adversary he feared had slipped through his fingers, Holmes was seizing the opportunity to confront him directly and so force him to show his hand.

Moriarty merely tilted his head slightly to the left and set the pen aside. 'I am familiar with some of these incidents from the newspaper accounts, of course, but I had no direct involvement in any of them.'

'Direct no,' Holmes acknowledged, 'but through the agency of numerous intermediaries, catspaws, bogus companies and other devices, I believe I can detect a trail leading to your door.'

Their eyes met, Holmes's steely gaze pressing hard upon Moriarty's studied indifference. I almost fancied I could feel the air crackling between them. After a lengthy silence the professor spoke.

'I will confess this much: that I have from time to time made investments, the profit of which was contingent upon the outcome of certain events. You, Mr Holmes, have on occasion seen fit to involve yourself in those events to the detriment of my fortunes. Yes, I have been aware of your presence, like a mouse nibbling at the edge of a tapestry.'

The last words were uttered with a sneer that bordered on the malevolent.

'You underestimate me, professor,' said Holmes. 'Like you I have my agents, my informers, sources of information which are unknown even to you. I have been accumulating a comprehensive dossier that requires only a few minor details to reach completion.'

For a moment Moriarty's whole body seemed to swell like the hood of a cobra, and it was only with a visible effort that he was able to draw a deep breath and relax.

'Well, I see that you have taken an extraordinary interest in my activities, Mr Holmes. You flatter me.'

'I assure you that was not my intention.'

Moriarty waved a careless hand in my direction. 'If we are to discuss matters of so delicate a nature, perhaps it would be better if Dr Watson were to absent himself.'

Before Holmes could utter a word I spoke up firmly. 'Under no circumstances will I do so.'

Professor Moriarty regarded me steadily for a few seconds, his eyebrows slightly upraised. 'Very well then, let us proceed. If you have something to say to me, Mr Holmes, do please go ahead and say it.'

Holmes settled back in his chair. 'I imagine, professor, that you can anticipate much of what I am going to say.'

'Indeed I can.' The professor targeted Holmes with a look as deadly as a rifle shot. 'You have already stated that you have been gathering evidence against me. When your case is complete I suppose that you intend to spring the trap and hand me over to agents of the law.'

'Very good, professor,' Holmes congratulated him. 'I couldn't have put it better myself. And you in your turn will tell me that not only will my efforts prove futile but that if I persist I do so at the hazard of my life.'

'Exactly. I hope you don't think it ill-mannered of me to resort to anything so crude as a threat.'

'Not at all, professor. I take it as a compliment.'

'It is intended as such, but also as a sincere warning. It would pain me to see an intellect such as yours needlessly destroyed just as much as if I saw an exquisite Ming vase of the Xuande period shattered in an act of thuggish desecration.'

'I am afraid, professor, that my feelings in this matter differ radically from your own. Not only would I rejoice in your destruction, I would willingly sacrifice my own life to achieve that end.'

This appeared to give Moriarty a moment's pause, but eventually he summoned a thin smile. 'Let us hope it does not come to that for the present, for I believe our country needs us both.'

Holmes raised a sardonic eyebrow. 'I would never have guessed that you cared so much for the welfare of the nation.'

'Believe me, Mr Holmes, my desire to see the defeat of Germany is just as strong as your own,' Moriarty stated gravely. 'In a society such as ours, a man like me has the full protection of the law, no matter what accusations you choose to bring against me. In the state favoured by Herr Hitler, a man can be arrested on a whim and shot without the bother of a trial. I would feel uncomfortable under such a regime. Therefore I am happy to work towards its destruction.'

'I have no doubt you have made yourself indispensable,' said Holmes. 'In truth, I cannot imagine a brain better suited to the cracking of the enemy codes than your own.'

Moriarty acknowledged the compliment with a small nod. 'You also have some reputation as a breaker of ciphers.' He plucked a sheet of typed paper from his desk. 'This message has just come into our possession. I would be interested to hear what you make of it.'

He handed the sheet to Holmes, who examined it through narrowed eyes before passing it to me. At first glance all I saw was a series of unintelligible numbers.

3	2	17	1
5	1	5	4
2	4	12	3
10	2	6	1
6	3	8	5
3	7	15	2
1	2	0	5

'Well, Holmes, have you anything to say?' There was no disguising the oily challenge in Moriarty's words.

'Only that once you have a copy of Wednesday's London *Times* before you,' Holmes replied carelessly, 'deciphering the message will be child's play.'

The professor's surprise was evident, though he made every effort to suppress it.

'Holmes,' I said, 'the arrangement of numbers does remind me of the book cipher with which you were presented when tackling the Curse of the Sandervilles. But beyond that . . .'

The merest twitch of the lips betrayed Holmes's distaste at the colourful title I had assigned to that case. 'In that instance it was a specific edition of *Robinson Crusoe* that was the key, the numbers in the cipher referring to the page, the line and the word. In this case, however we must be dealing with a most unusual book, one that has no more than ten pages.'

I tapped the paper with my forefinger. 'Yes, I see. The first column of numbers refers to the page of a newspaper, not a book, the second to columns on that page, the third to lines and the last to the position of the word within that line. But *The Times*?' I puzzled. 'How can you be so sure?'

'To fulfil its purpose this paper must be easily available, widely distributed, and cover a range of topics in order to provide an adequate vocabulary. Also *The Times* has eight pages in its Monday and Tuesday editions with ten pages as standard for the rest of the week, and each page is exactly seven columns across. It fits perfectly.'

'But by that logic,' I objected, 'the last row of numbers refers to a line zero, which makes no sense. And how do you know it's Wednesday's edition that is being used?'

'Ah, therein lies the brilliance of it,' Holmes declared admiringly. 'The sender has the choice of any recent edition and only needs to include a reference to the date.

The last line, as you have pointed out, is the only one to feature an anomalous zero.'

I handed the page back to him. 'And that is significant?'

'Well, any interloper attempting to interpret the cipher would assume the key to be in the first line rather than the last and so be misled. Those last numbers refer to a recent edition, the twelfth of May, or in other words, this past Wednesday.'

Moriarty clapped his hands quietly together. 'Bravo, Mr Holmes. I see your biographer has not exaggerated your gifts.'

'And now, professor,' said Holmes, tossing the paper back on to the desk, 'if we have finished playing games, might we come to the purpose of our visit – the so-called devil's blaze?'

8

HOUSE OF SECRETS

Moriarty raised one hand to examine his carefully manicured fingernails. 'Yes, the incendiary killings, which, I believe, have so far claimed four victims.'

'Correct,' said Holmes. 'You have, of course, been asked by the Intelligence Inner Council to personally scrutinise all recent intelligence reports for any clue to these murders.'

'Since one of their own was burned to death before their very eyes, they are naturally terrified for their own safety,' said Moriarty with a glint of amusement.

The obvious pleasure he took in the council's discomfiture I found utterly offensive. I inquired sharply, 'Have you then discovered any clue, professor?'

'I'm afraid I have no comfort to offer,' Moriarty respon-ded with no hint of regret. 'There is nowhere among all the chatter any word or phrase that even hints at a special incendiary device. Nor is there any reference to any of the victims. If this is a new German terror weapon, then they have shrouded the whole project in an unprecedented and impenetrable silence.'

'Are we to take it then that it is the work of a home-grown menace?' said Holmes. There was no doubting the meaning in the hard look he had fixed upon the professor.

Moriarty placed a hand upon his breast to signify his complete innocence. 'Me, Mr Holmes? That suspicion is unworthy of you. Why, even if I had possession of so flamboyant a means of destruction, what need of it would I have? Come, let me give you a tour of this establishment and show you the resources already at my command.'

Rising from his desk, he beckoned us towards the door. Holmes threw me a glance of mingled surprise and apprehension. He had not anticipated his enemy to be quite so accommodating. We followed the professor into the outer office where he issued some brisk instructions to his secretary before leading the way downstairs.

As we passed her desk, the receptionist raised her hand timidly, like a nervous pupil attracting the attention of a stern teacher.

'Yes?' Moriarty snapped.

'Professor, the First Lord of the Admiralty phoned.' The poor woman sounded as though she were apologising. 'He wants to arrange a meeting.'

Moriarty pursed his lips in irritation. 'Tell him I may be able to fit him in briefly on Monday, but no earlier. And see to it that all materials relating to the North Atlantic convoys are placed on my desk before I return.'

'Yes, sir, of course.' With a harried frown she reached for her telephone, no longer the cheerful gossip we had encountered on our arrival.

Once we were outside I was glad to feel the warmth of the sun on my face after the chilly atmosphere of Moriarty's office. Even out here the professor radiated a subtle, subliminal menace as tangible as an early frost. It was reassuring to see groups of ordinary human beings strolling along the winding paths and the messengers darting like minnows from hut to hut.

Two men, an RAF officer and a civilian with the air

of a scholar, passed us by. I heard the RAF man say, '*Konnichiwa, Rowbotham-san. O-genki desu ka?*'

To which the other responded, '*Hai, genki desu, Fincher-san. Anata wa?*'

I couldn't help turning back to look at them, wondering at their incomprehensible conversation.

'They're practising their Japanese,' Moriarty informed me. 'We had a devil of a time finding anyone who spoke it at all and we need more men to learn it. I will let you imagine the difficulty of breaking their codes, given that each word in their language is represented by a single symbol.'

He was about to enlighten us further on the subject of the Japanese ciphers when an approaching figure caught his eye. It was a husky, heavy-jawed man in an ill-fitting suit. As he marched directly towards us, his feet stamped the path as if the very ground offended him.

'Excuse me a moment, gentlemen,' Moriarty addressed us mildly. 'I must deal with this.'

He advanced to meet the newcomer in order to cut him off before he could reach us. The man's long, grey face seemed to twitch in habitual irritation. He raised a finger as the professor drew near, as though about to make a loud declaration, but before he could speak Moriarty gripped his upper arm and yanked him away. They repaired to a discreet distance with their backs towards us, talking in low voices.

I took the opportunity to exchange a few words with Holmes.

'Are you absolutely certain that this man is the evil mastermind you believe is the source of so much crime?

I admit there is something unlikeable about him, but would so dangerous a man really be placed in charge of an establishment as sensitive as this?'

Holmes allowed himself an ironic shake of the head. 'It would take a mind more perspicacious than any politician's to penetrate the barriers of falsehood with which Professor Moriarty has surrounded himself. Even I took years to follow the slender trail that led to his Oxford college and the humble study from which he supervised some of the most villainous schemes in history.'

I glanced over to where the professor was engaged in a hushed but intense conversation with the sour-looking man. 'So why this tour, Holmes? Why should he want to reveal any of his secrets to us?'

'He wishes to demonstrate to me the extent of his power,' said Holmes, eyeing his adversary from afar, 'and to show that he is entirely unassailable in this fortress of his.'

At that moment Moriarty parted from his colleague with a dismissive gesture and walked back towards us. The other man stalked off with a scowl and disappeared behind the great house.

'I apologise, gentlemen,' said our host. 'Professor Kilbane does valuable work for us, but on occasion feels he has the right to impose upon my time.'

'So that is Professor Kilbane of Edinburgh University,' said Holmes, 'well known for his work on Fibonacci sequences.'

'Indeed,' Moriarty affirmed. 'He is no doubt a man of some ability, but tends to a troublesome irascibility when placed under pressure. Now if you will please follow me.'

As he led the way into the nearest of the long wooden huts, I wondered what sort of pressure Moriarty was placing upon his colleague. From the outside the hut had the appearance of having been hastily constructed, and was so homely one might have expected to find a troop of boy scouts inside mastering their knot-tying.

Signalling us to silence, the professor opened the door. When we entered we beheld row upon row of modern radio sets buzzing upon their tables while an operator in military uniform hunched intently over each one, their faces creased in concentration beneath their headphones. The air was filled with the hot tang of electronic current and the vibratory hum of the antennae. I saw one operator rip a sheet from the pad he was scribbling on and wave it in the air until a supervisor plucked it from his fingers. The paper was then handed to a messenger who disappeared out of the door.

Moriarty, clearly, was very much in his element. 'This is just one of our communications centres,' he informed us proudly as he led us back outside. 'My operatives gather everything from coded military messages to careless hearsay. Why, when Herr Hitler's bathwater is insufficiently warm, I am the first to hear of it other than those within immediate range of his ire.'

'No doubt his bathing habits have their influence on more significant events,' Holmes commented.

'Every fragment of information is of value to a mind capable of extrapolating from the small to the large,' said Moriarty. 'Even requisitions of tinned beef or the planning of a band concert might provide clues to the movement of troops or the location of senior officers.'

The next hut was filled with the deafening clatter of dozens of teleprinters, all of them operated by young women. I wondered how they were able to tolerate the din until I saw that some of them had plugs of wax stuffed into their ears. My own ears were still ringing from the noise when we emerged into the fresh air.

We proceeded to a third hut. 'In here,' said Moriarty, opening the door, 'is something rather special.'

The room beyond was occupied by a score of wooden cabinets, each about eight feet tall and seven feet wide, filled with rows of coloured circular drums which whirred and clicked incessantly. The noise was not unlike the clickety-clack of knitting needles, though magnified many times over. Each machine was attended by a Wren with a pair of tweezers, making delicate adjustments to the wiring with all the care of a devoted surgical nurse.

'These are our Bombe machines,' the professor explained. 'They are based upon a Polish prototype and can test combinations of numbers and letters at a speed far in excess of any human capability.'

In spite of Moriarty's evident pride, they appeared to me to be nothing more than elaborate adding machines.

'I think,' said Holmes, 'they will never match the other qualities of the human mind.'

'Perhaps, Mr Holmes,' said Moriarty in cold mockery, 'you are apprehensive that a mere mechanism might one day exceed the capacity of your own vaunted intellect.'

Holmes did not bother to raise his voice above the clatter of the machines in reply. Once outside he said, 'From some of the notable persons I have observed hereabout, professor, your human resources are also formidable.'

'You may judge that for yourself,' said Moriarty.

He grimaced as he opened the door to the next hut and waved away the cloud of pipe smoke that billowed out. Dotted around the big open room were clusters of men of academic appearance, some hunched around tables, others gathered before blackboards covered with strings of letters and numbers. The air was filled with the hum of animated discussion. I caught a few phrases such as *reverse substitution* and *Weltraum sequence* before the professor led us away, stifling a cough as he did so.

'Some of our code-breakers seem unable to function without the aid of stimulants,' he said, 'so I indulge them as long as they produce the necessary results.'

'And what do you keep in that blockhouse over there?' Holmes inquired, pointing to a great concrete building three storeys high that lay several hundred yards to the north.

'Oh, I am afraid, Mr Holmes, that even you are not permitted access to that particular area of our establishment.' Moriarty seemed unpleasantly pleased to have the opportunity to deny Holmes's curiosity. 'Its contents are far too sensitive.'

Holmes merely raised an eyebrow and shrugged. 'Well, professor, I suppose we all have some secrets we prefer to keep to ourselves.'

'I do have another place of interest to show you,' the professor offered in a tone of mock conciliation. 'As I am sure you will appreciate, even the most active intellects sometimes require diversion of the non-mental kind, which is why we have this well-equipped gymnasium.'

He led us into a low wooden building where we

immediately beheld all the standard equipment used for physical exercise: a vaulting horse, parallel bars, climbing ropes and frames, punching bags and other such items. At the far end of the room a rugged figure stood alone on a fencing piste directing a series of energetic sword thrusts into the empty air. As we approached he turned and saluted us with his rapier.

He wore military boots and trousers but had removed his tunic and rolled up his sleeves. His brown hair was greying at the temples and a bushy russet moustache bracketed his square, hard-set jaw. He watched us with the sharpened eyes of a huntsman.

'Mr Holmes, Dr Watson,' said Professor Moriarty, 'allow me to introduce you to my head of security – Colonel Sebastian Moran.'

9

CROSSED SWORDS

I failed to suppress a start of recognition. Now that I heard the name I recognised those bullish, arrogant features. I had encountered Moran during the Great War when he was a junior officer. Even then he had a reputation for brutality and was reputed to treat his own men as harshly as he would the enemy. I recalled how he roundly and regularly cursed the orderlies attending him when he was laid up in the infirmary with a deep bayonet wound. There was even a rumour that he had shot a pair of German prisoners after engineering their escape to provide himself with a spot of hunting.

'Holmes and Watson, eh?' He casually slashed the air with the tip of his sword as he spoke. 'Private snoopers, ain't you? Funny to find you prying about here.'

'The Intelligence Inner Council sent Mr Holmes here,' Moriarty explained, 'to inquire into a matter that has set them astir.'

'It don't take much to put a scare into those pasty-faced Whitehall johnnies.' Moran gave vent to a croaking laugh.

'Practising alone, I see,' Holmes observed.

'I made short work of a couple of young sprats before you arrived,' bragged Moran. 'Taught them a lesson or two then packed them off back to their duties.'

'Colonel Moran has assembled his own force to

preserve the security of Hunterswood,' Moriarty told us.

'The Special Action Brigade,' said Moran. 'You'll hear us called the Sabres for short.'

'Very dashing, I'm sure,' I remarked. 'But perhaps we should be moving on.' Though he did not appear to remember me, I found Moran's company as disagreeable as ever and had no wish to linger.

We were turning to leave when Moran barked, 'I say, Holmes, there's a rumour you were a bit of a swordsman in your day.'

'In my day?' Holmes repeated. 'I hope I am not yet in the evening of my years.'

'Then why don't you prove it?' Moran challenged him with an evil twist of his mouth. 'Pit yourself against me now. Unless you've got too rusty.'

Knowing Moran's ruthless ways of old, I was not going to allow my friend to place himself in danger. 'Really, Moran, we are here on serious business,' I told him, 'not to play games.'

'Ah, so Watson is here as a protector,' Moran suggested sneeringly. 'Treats you as one of his patients, eh, Mr Holmes?'

Holmes was unruffled. 'I need no protection, but Dr Watson is correct. This is no time for sports.'

'Oh, come, Mr Holmes,' said Moriarty in his oiliest voice, 'surely it would do no harm to indulge Colonel Moran. We could place a gentleman's wager on the bout – just to make it interesting.'

'Yes, a wager,' Moran concurred. 'Go ahead, Holmes – you can name the stakes.'

I saw the side of my friend's mouth quirk as it often

did when an intriguing thought occurred to him. 'Are you agreeable to that, professor?'

'Of course,' Moriarty acquiesced. 'We're all allies here, are we not?'

There was no mistaking the intended irony in that statement and I felt sure that Holmes was being lured into some sort of trap.

'Really, Holmes—' I protested, but he cut me off with an upraised hand.

'In that case,' he said, 'I accept the challenge but on the sole condition that in the event of my victory you, professor, will give me access to that bombproof building whose contents you are so desirous to conceal.'

Moran grinned broadly at the prospect of a fight while Moriarty slowly nodded in appreciation of how Holmes had contrived to turn the situation to his advantage.

'I see that like me, Mr Holmes, you understand that information is the most valuable currency of all. Very well, but you must offer something worthy in return.' Moriarty tapped his chin with a pale, well-manicured finger. 'Yes, I know. In the event you lose the bout, you must tell me a secret of your own.'

'And what might that be?' Holmes inquired lightly.

Moriarty had about him the predatory air of a fox slinking through a hen house. 'There was that period from nineteen thirty-five to six when you seemed to vanish from the face of the Earth. Some attributed this to your final demise, claiming your death had been covered up to prevent a resultant upsurge in crime. But of course, you returned hale and hearty, claiming that you had simply been travelling to broaden your mind.'

'Is that not explanation enough?' I intervened.

'By no means, doctor,' Moriarty responded sharply. 'Yes, Mr Holmes, I would be fascinated to learn the true story behind your mysterious absence. Is that not a fair wager?'

I was horrified at the prospect of Holmes's being compelled to expose to this man a secret so dark and painful that he had revealed it to me only a few months before on the understanding that I would share it with no one.

'Holmes, this is going too far,' I declared. 'Let us return to London and continue the investigation there.'

Holmes gave no sign of having heard me but addressed Moriarty with calm confidence. 'Perfectly fair, professor.' He turned to Moran. 'Shall we keep it simple, colonel? One square hit to the torso for the win, no other hits counting?'

'That'll make for a dashed short contest,' said Moran with a wolfish smile. 'But if that's all you're up to, Holmes, then so be it.'

'I'm sure that will suffice,' Moriarty concurred. 'After all, it is only a friendly bit of sport.'

While I would hardly have described it as friendly, I was relieved it was not to be an extended bout. My friend was spry and quick for his age, but Moran bristled with such a brutish animal energy that it would be hard to fend him off for any length of time.

My concern increased when Holmes moved towards the padded vests and mesh masks hanging on the wall and Moran waved him back.

'Come, Holmes,' he scoffed, 'the blades are guarded.' He tapped the protective leather cap inlaid with cork that was fixed upon the point of his sword. 'Not scared of a bruise or two, are you?'

'Not at all, colonel, not at all,' said Holmes, backing away.

As he was removing his jacket and rolling up his sleeves, I drew him aside to where Moriarty and Moran would not overhear.

'Did you not notice?' I asked in an urgent whisper. 'Moran hasn't a drop of sweat on him. He wasn't fencing anyone before we arrived. He's been lying here in wait.'

'Quite so,' my friend agreed unconcernedly. 'Moriarty arranged all of this beforehand in order to test me.'

I could hardly believe that he was taking the matter so lightly. 'Look, I know Moran of old, and though he may wear a veneer of civilisation, underneath he's a sheer savage. You can't trust him an inch.'

Holmes eyed his opponent, who was stretching his limbs and stabbing the air with his rapier. 'I shall certainly bear that in mind.'

'But Holmes, is it worth the risk to yourself? You can still walk away from this.'

Holmes was resolute. 'Now that we have penetrated the dragon's cave, we surely cannot leave without taking at least one piece of treasure from his hoard.'

He selected a weapon for himself from a rack on the wall and made some experimental passes. After allowing the combatants another minute to warm themselves up, Moriarty drew them together.

'Gentlemen, I am sure you are aware of the rules,' he said in a didactic tone. 'Only a direct hit to the torso with the point of the blade scores a win. A hit to any other part of the body is considered a foul stroke. Three of those amounts to a disqualification and therefore victory for the other fencer. Are we agreed?'

Both men nodded, and at the professor's instruction of '*En garde!*' stepped back to assume the standard fencing posture. They faced each other side on with the sword presented in the right hand, the left arm tucked behind.

'Very well,' said Moriarty. 'Begin!'

Both men inched cautiously forward, though Moran's advance was the more aggressive. I saw Holmes's eyes fixed upon his opponent with the same intensity I had seen so many times when he scrutinised a crucial piece of evidence. All at once Moran made a probing thrust which Holmes deflected before countering with a stroke of his own. This forced Moran to take a backward step to avoid a hit and raise his blade into a defensive position. With a wordless grunt he resumed his attack, beating at Holmes's sword in an effort to loosen his grip on the hilt. The twin blades rasped around each other in a communal spiral and both men pressed forward until the guards were grinding together. Their eyes locked, Holmes's firmly focused, Moran's flaring with the crude joy of battle.

The colonel exerted his sheer bulk and with a grating cry threw my friend back a step. Holmes quickly recovered and parried the incoming attack with a deft turn of his blade. Falling into a crouch, Moran dropped his rapier under Holmes's guard and drove the blunted point of the weapon hard into his opponent's thigh.

A twitch of pain touched my friend's lips as Moriarty called, 'Halt!'

Moran drew back with a grin of malevolent satisfaction.

'Are you able to continue, Mr Holmes?' Moriarty inquired with unconvincing solicitude.

'As Colonel Moran predicted earlier,' said Holmes, 'it is merely a bruise.'

In spite of his dismissive attitude, given the force behind the thrust I had no doubt that it hurt like the very devil.

'That was an off-target hit by you, colonel,' Moriarty chided. 'You must aim for the proper target.'

Moran made no acknowledgement of the warning as he and Holmes resumed the *en garde* position.

'Again!' said the professor, initiating a resumption of the contest.

This time Moran threw himself immediately into a ferocious assault, probing and thrusting in an effort to force a path through Holmes's persistent defence. Finally one of his strokes was only barely deflected. The covered point of his sword slid over Holmes's bare arm, but the steely edge of the blade cut a bloody groove in the exposed flesh.

Again Moriarty called a halt and both men withdrew.

'Mr Holmes, you are wounded,' Moriarty observed with no pretence of sympathy.

'It is nothing,' Holmes responded, barely even glancing at the injury.

'Here, let me look at that,' I insisted, stepping around the professor. Though he was irked at the intervention, Holmes allowed me to examine the cut.

'This is quite deep,' I told him, 'and needs to be treated.'

'There is a first aid kit in the corner over there,' Moriarty pointed out. 'Do you wish to retire, Mr Holmes?'

'By no means,' said Holmes, shrugging off my attentions. 'You can tend to it later, Watson, once the bout is over.'

Reluctantly I backed away as the professor signalled the resumption of the contest. The sight of blood appeared to fill Moran with a renewed fury and he charged forward like a maddened bull. I knew now that he was capable of any savagery and that Sherlock Holmes was in the utmost danger.

10

A DOORWAY INTO THE FUTURE

Moran had to be aware that one more off-target hit would hand the victory to Holmes, but I could not tell if his aim was to win the contest or to inflict an even more grievous injury on his opponent. The ferocity with which he now wielded his blade in a series of rapid thrusts and cuts was as unnerving as facing the snapping jaws of a monstrous reptile. Holmes was beginning to display signs of fatigue – a sheen of perspiration on his large brow, his breathing quick and shallow. And yet his defence held firm while Moran's assault grew more and more frenzied.

At last it appeared that the colonel was tiring himself out and Holmes began to force him back with a series of skilful counter-strokes. Moran uttered a guttural growl of frustration, his face suffused with crimson, his chest swelling with unconstrained rage. Finally his frustration boiled over and he aimed a cruel slash at Holmes's face.

My friend, however, had clearly anticipated this un-lawful blow and sidestepped it nimbly. Thrown off balance by his own momentum, Moran was caught entirely by surprise when Holmes slammed a knee into his heaving belly, knocking the breath out of him. He then cracked the guard of his sword-hilt down hard on the colonel's wrist, forcing him to drop his weapon with a snarl of pain.

As Moran rounded on his opponent, Holmes extended his arm and pressed the point of his sword decisively on the centre of the colonel's chest.

'A winning hit, I believe,' he noted drily.

For an instant we were all frozen in position until Holmes stepped back and lowered his blade. At once Moran snatched up his sword, seized hold of the leather covering on the point and flung it away.

'Come on, let's have at it again with naked steel!' he roared. 'Let's see who draws first blood!'

'Moran, command yourself!' Moriarty's voice had lost its silken edge and cracked the air like a bullwhip.

Moran glared at his chief and seethed for a moment like a storm cloud pulsing with thunderbolts. Then he cast his sword clattering to the floor and snatched his jacket from its peg. He stabbed a finger in Holmes's direction.

'You will face me again, Holmes!' he threatened.

'I have no doubt of that,' Holmes responded coolly as he placed his own weapon back on its rack.

Moran treated us all to a final, simmering glower and stalked out of the building.

'My apologies, gentlemen,' said the professor, resuming his usual suave manner. 'Colonel Moran is a man of strong passions.'

'That much is evident,' I observed. I could feel the threat of violence still throbbing in the air like the vibration of a huge gong.

'Such ferocity is a quality to be valued in a watchdog,' Holmes commented, 'but not in a gentleman.'

I made him sit down while I fetched the first aid kit. I cleaned the cut in his forearm, dabbed it with a disinfectant and wrapped it tightly in a bandage. When I was done he slid back into his jacket and straightened it with a tug, as if to reestablish an atmosphere of civilised restraint.

'Our wager, professor,' he prompted.

'Of course, Mr Holmes,' Moriarty responded mildly. 'I am a man of my word. Otherwise I could not carry on my business.'

As we walked together towards the secretive edifice, I could not help but note that Moriarty's earlier reluctance to grant us admission had been replaced by an almost gleeful anticipation. In contrast to the innocent, makeshift appearance of the wooden huts, this great concrete block had the rigid impenetrability of a fortress designed to withstand a full-scale military assault.

The entrance was guarded by two sentries, each of whom wore a shoulder patch displaying the emblem of a curved sword. These I assumed were two members of Moran's Special Action Brigade. Even though we were accompanied by the director of Hunterswood, they eyed us with hostility before giving way to him as he pushed open the heavy steel door.

Beyond was a passage lit with a harsh electric light. An efficient-looking woman of middle years in horn-rimmed spectacles was seated at a desk at the far end of the passage. Jumping to her feet, she said, 'Professor Moriarty. Shall I inform Professor Kilbane you are here?'

'No need.' Moriarty waved her back into her chair. 'He is expecting me.'

He took us through a stout oak door into a chamber larger than any we had yet seen, which was occupied by the most extraordinary mechanism I had ever beheld.

It resembled a huge steel-cased cabinet, the bulk of which occupied fully two-thirds of the room, towering up to within a few inches of the ceiling. To its right, rows of lights flashed red and white to the clicking of unseen switches. In the centre, interconnecting networks of wire were linked to an array of tiny plugholes, much as in a telephone switchboard. Below this was a teleprinter, while to the left long ribbons of tape swished and spun around large metallic drums.

'Gentlemen,' Moriarty announced, 'I present you with the future.'

Professor Kilbane was studying a stream of ticker tape that was chattering out of a small slot at the far left of the machine. When he looked round, his sour features contorted into an expression of even greater displeasure at the sight of us. I wondered how he tolerated working here with the constant clatter and buzzing of the enormous machine. In addition to the noise, it gave off a stifling heat which the ventilation ducts in the ceiling did little to dissipate.

'It is certainly the largest calculator I have ever beheld,' said Holmes, removing his hat and fanning himself with it.

Moriarty appeared somewhat miffed by this remark. 'I think at the very least we might refer to it as a super-calculator. We have given it the name Velox.'

I retained enough of my school Latin to recognise that the name meant swift, being the root of our word velocity. This was doubtless a reference to the speed of its operations. 'I'm sure it tots up numbers at an impressive rate,' I said, 'but it is still merely an adding machine, not a doorway into the future.'

'Your lack of imagination does you discredit, doctor,' Moriarty retorted with a sharp edge to his voice. 'Unlike any mere counting machine, Velox works to a programme via electronic valve pulses and delicate, complex circuits. It processes information at a rate hitherto undreamed.'

'And yet it still requires the services of a human operator,' Holmes pointed out, nodding in the direction of Professor Kilbane, who continued to glower at us even while scrutinising the machine's printout.

An expression of abstract thought passed across Moriarty's features. 'That too may one day be dispensed with.'

Kilbane dropped the tape he was holding and strode towards us.

'Velox carries out its calculations with an unprecedented rapidity, far outstripping the capacity of the human brain,' he informed us snappishly. 'It enables us to crack in a matter of weeks a cipher it would otherwise have taken years to solve. Compared to Velox a room full of Bombe machines is about as effectual as an abacus.'

'The initial design was Professor Kilbane's,' said Moriarty, 'though I flatter myself that I have contributed a number of improvements to its operation.'

'Really, professor, I was under the impression that no visitors were allowed into this building,' Kilbane complained, waving a hand in our direction as though to dispel a displeasing odour.

'Mr Sherlock Holmes is a special case,' said Moriarty. 'His is one of the few intellects large enough to appreciate what we have accomplished here.'

'I am certainly impressed by the huge advances you have made in the science of code-breaking,' said Holmes.

'Code-breaking?' snorted Moriarty. 'That is merely the beginning. But come, gentlemen, we have distracted Professor Kilbane long enough.'

He opened the door for us, but as we passed through Kilbane caught him by the arm and muttered something about valves.

Moriarty shook himself loose with a testy shrug. 'Yes, professor, we shall discuss that shortly.'

'I am sure there is no need to remind you of the absolute confidentiality required of any visitor to Hunterswood,' said Moriarty as we left the concrete blockhouse behind us. He fixed Holmes with the cold gaze of an adder. 'Were you to breathe any word of what you have seen here or disclose the names of any of our personnel, myself included, you would find yourself placed under immediate arrest and confined to a prison of the most uncomfortable sort.'

'You may be assured, professor,' Holmes responded affably, 'that I will do nothing to cause you distress with regard to your very valuable work here.'

'And beyond that?' The icy glare did not waver.

'As regards those other matters, I believe we have both made our intentions clear.'

The professor nodded like a man accepting the conditions of a duel. 'I will leave you to make your own way back to your car. I have to discuss some further adjustments to Velox with Professor Kilbane.'

'We certainly do not wish to keep you from your work,' said Holmes.

Moriarty started to turn away, then paused. 'Would you mind, however, if I offered you a word of advice concerning this business you are investigating?'

'I'm sure I would appreciate whatever insights you might have to offer,' said Holmes, 'from your unique perspective.'

'Quite.' Moriarty clasped his hands behind his back and spoke thoughtfully. 'Consider this, then: if the aim is merely to kill these men, why not use one of the usual methods, say, a bullet from a sniper's rifle, or a discreetly administered poison?'

'You have my full attention, professor. Please continue.'

'For my own part I would not dream of using such a flamboyant, not to say garish, method of execution, save for one purpose: to make an example of the victims.'

Holmes nodded slowly. 'That is a point worth considering.'

'Well, good luck to you, Mr Holmes,' said Moriarty, turning away. 'In this case, at least.'

He walked briskly back to the concrete building and disappeared inside.

'Well, Watson, this has proved a most informative visit,' Holmes declared as we followed a path around the west wing of the main house.

'Really, Holmes? We have learned nothing concerning those incendiary deaths.'

'No, but we have learned a good deal about Professor Moriarty, and have perhaps garnered a few clues to his future intentions.'

As we came in view of the driveway, we saw Jane Garrick leaning on the bonnet of the saloon car. She straightened up smartly at the sight of us and smiled a greeting.

'Are you ready to return to London, gentlemen?'

'More than ready,' I assured her.

Once we were settled into the back seat, she drove us through the gate and on to the southbound road.

'I'm afraid we're not permitted to stop anywhere for lunch,' Jane Garrick informed us, 'so I had the canteen put a few things together for you. They're in that knapsack at your feet.'

Looking down, I saw the pack and, suddenly conscious of my hunger, I bent to pick it up. Even as I placed it in my lap, our driver slid shut the glass screen, effectively cutting off any further attempt at conversation.

'She may not have much to say to us, Watson,' commented Holmes with an amused twinkle, 'but she has not neglected our appetites.'

Inside the knapsack I found some corned beef sandwiches wrapped in wax paper, two tin cups and a Thermos flask filled with hot tea. Holmes accepted a cup of tea and sipped at it meditatively.

'And now, Holmes,' I suggested, 'perhaps you can tell me more of this remarkable man you believe to be the world's greatest criminal.'

PART TWO
Avalon

11

THE ARK OF TRUTH

Wren Garrick piloted the saloon smoothly southward, past fields and hedgerows bright with the colours of summer. With the glass panel between us and our driver, Holmes and I were able to converse without being overheard. While I bit into my first sandwich, Holmes proceeded to acquaint me with the career of his most dangerous adversary.

'Robert James Moriarty, born in Belfast in 1883, is the eldest of three brothers,' he began. 'The middle name James is their mother's maiden name and is common to all three brothers. The second, Ronald, is an officer serving with our forces in the Far East. Roger, the youngest, is a stationmaster in Suffolk.

'Even at school it was evident that Robert Moriarty was endowed by nature with a phenomenal mathematical faculty. At Oxford his peers were as amazed by his intellectual brilliance as they were discomfited by the coldness of his manner. It was not uncommon for him to berate his colleagues for their lack of comprehension of what he saw as the most fundamental concepts.'

Holmes paused to refresh himself with a sip of tea before continuing.

'He first came to prominence through his elaboration of the Cayley-Kline metrics used for non-Euclidean geometry. His reputation was further elevated by a groundbreaking work on the theoretical structure of hyperspace. A few years later he published *Causes and Effects in Higher Mathematics*, in which he asserted that logic and mathematics are one and the same and should form the guiding principles of an advanced society.'

'I'm surprised so prominent an academic would have the time and privacy to carry on the criminal activities you spoke of,' I commented between bites of my sandwich.

'Moriarty's eminence was such that he could decline to do any teaching, restricting himself to pure research,' Holmes explained. 'So abstruse was his work that he needed no colleagues to assist in his studies, and so powerful was his intellect that he could carry out those researches while simultaneously supervising plots of the most devious criminality. There was no one close enough to him to notice anything untoward in his life as he has a natural disinclination for the company of others.'

I could not help but reflect that Holmes's own circle of intimate acquaintances was also severely limited, scarcely extending beyond myself and his brother Mycroft. Pushing that thought to one side, I said, 'So now he commands the government's most secret and vital intelligence installation.'

'Yes, and with the most wide-ranging information network in history at his beck and call,' said Holmes, 'the potential for extending his influence through blackmail and bribery is practically unlimited.'

'And guarding his stronghold is the most brutal officer I have ever encountered in all my long years.'

'The name Sebastian Moran was not entirely unknown to me,' said Holmes. 'Some years ago I connected him to the death of Lord Radford, which, by a concatenation of events, led to a large fortune's pouring into Professor Moriarty's well-concealed coffers. I was not, however, aware that their association had become quite so close.'

'Holmes, do you think that Moriarty himself might be behind these ghastly killings?'

'He is more than capable of it,' Holmes conceded, 'but his denial of any knowledge regarding them struck me as, for him, unusually candid. I do not doubt that he has aims of his own that are nothing to do with the defence of this country, but I do not see that his interests would be served in any way by the elimination of those particular men.'

'Did you notice Professor Kilbane attempting to detain him?' I asked. 'I'm sure I heard him demand that they have an urgent discussion about valves. He seemed quite agitated about the subject.'

'Not valves, Watson,' said Holmes, whose hearing was always more acute than mine. 'Professor Kilbane wished to discuss something called Avalon.'

'Avalon?' I repeated. 'Why on earth should two men engaged in such vital scientific work think it important to discuss some obscure aspect of Arthurian romance?'

'That is indeed a fascinating question,' said Holmes, 'though not one pertinent to our current investigation.'

I finished off the last bite of my sandwich and sighed. 'Then we are as much at sea as ever.'

'Perhaps not.' Holmes appeared to be in no way discouraged. 'If any lawbreaker in the land was at the root of this horror, the professor would know, so we can rule out the possibility that these acts are merely criminal. And I believe him when he says there has been no reference to these deaths in the communications of the enemy.'

I drummed my fingers on my armrest. 'So if they are not the acts of criminals or of enemy agents, where does that leave us?'

'The elimination of large categories of suspects is always a first step,' Holmes reminded me. 'The next step will be to probe for a motive.'

'Moriarty suggested that the victims were being made an example of,' I recalled. 'I cannot help but think of those pamphlets Lestrade brought to our attention.'

Holmes nodded. 'Ah, the evangelical tracts of Miss Ophelia Faith.'

'These spectacular deaths appear to serve her purposes rather well,' I suggested. 'Is it possible she has somehow acquired the ability to punish men she regards as sinners and so advance her cause?'

'As you say, she would seem to have a motive,' Holmes agreed. 'I believe we should pay her a visit and assess whether or not she has the means.'

'Yes, I suppose we must,' I concurred, though the prospect was not an inviting one. I could only imagine the author of those fiery tracts to be a grim, hatchet-faced fanatic of the most unappealing sort.

So it was that the next morning we found ourselves standing outside a building which a sign over the door proclaimed to be The Ark of Truth. In the course of seeking out the address we learned that it had once been a dance hall, though it was now consecrated to a higher purpose. Pinned to the door was a poster depicting an angel hovering protectively over London with a quote from Psalm 124 in bright yellow letters:

> *If it had not been the Lord who was on our side then the waters had overwhelmed us, the stream had gone over our head. Our help is in the name of the Lord who made heaven and earth.*

Finding the door unlatched, we let ourselves in and walked down a short corridor to another door which opened with a creak. We stepped into a large meeting hall where about three dozen folding chairs were set up in rows facing a raised stage behind which hung a large wooden cross. Vases of flowers had been strategically placed so that they were illumined in the sunshine streaming through the skylights. A boy of about ten years old was sweeping the floor while a girl of a similar age was laying out hymn books on the chairs.

Holmes cleared his throat to attract their attention and they turned towards him, wide-eyed. Whether they recognised the great detective or whether his appearance alone was enough to strike them dumb, they stared as though some other-worldly apparition had materialised in their midst.

Holmes addressed them gently. 'Excuse us for disturbing you, but can you tell us where we might find Miss Ophelia Faith?'

The children continued to gape in silence, but the boy pointed to a door at the rear of the hall.

'We are very much obliged to you,' said Holmes, doffing his hat.

I could feel the eyes of the two youngsters following us as we walked down the length of the room, and only when we passed through the doorway did the sounds of sweeping and the slap of books on chairs resume.

We entered a spotlessly clean kitchen where once again many vases of flowers were in evidence. Two ladies were seated at a small table taking morning tea together. One of them I took to be Miss Ophelia Faith, but I was astonished to recognise the woman seated opposite her.

'Ah, Mr Holmes, Dr Watson.' Dr MacReady greeted us with a flourish of her teacup. 'I expected that you would drop by sooner or later.'

'Well, this is a busy morning!' Ophelia Faith declared brightly. 'First Mac drops in out of the blue and now two famous investigators.'

'Mac is what they used to call me at Lady Anne's School for Young Gentlewomen,' Dr MacReady explained with a toss of her head. 'Honestly, you'd think I was the only Scottish lass there.'

'You weren't the only one,' laughed Miss Faith, 'but you were definitely the most Scottish.'

In contrast to the tall, handsome Dr MacReady, the lady evangelist was petite and pretty with only a few threads of grey in her chestnut curls. The impish expression on her pert, rosy face bespoke a sweetness of nature I had not anticipated.

'Can I offer you gentlemen a drop of tea?' she asked, placing a hand on the china teapot.

'There are jam biscuits too,' Dr MacReady pointed out, taking a small bite from the one in her hand. 'I tell you frankly, they're so good, they taste of the old days before the war.'

'One of my congregation is a baker,' Miss Faith confided, 'and he knows I've got a bit of a sweet tooth.'

'Thank you, but no,' said Holmes. 'We've already had an adequate breakfast.'

'Yes, we are fine,' I felt compelled to agree, though the biscuits did look extremely appetising.

Ophelia Faith rose and smoothed down her sprig-flowered frock before beginning to gather the tea things on to a tray.

'So you were schoolmates?' I hazarded.

'Yes, in the very same year,' Dr MacReady confirmed. 'But it's been ages since we last saw each other.'

'Oh, the things we used to get up to in those days,' Miss Faith chortled. She placed a hand over her pert little mouth to suppress her mirth.

Dr MacReady grinned at the reminiscence. 'Who would've thought that Phoebe Puckering, the wee minx who hid out for three days on the school roof while the whole place was searching for her, would one day transform herself into Ophelia Faith, the fearless and respectable preacher?'

'I think the time Mac the Menace sneaked a stink bomb into the staff room gave us some indication of *your* future career,' countered Miss Faith with mock severity.

Holmes and I exchanged nonplussed glances as we tried to imagine these ladies, a scientist and an evangelist, as a pair of mischievous schoolgirls.

'Might I ask what brought about this happy reunion?' Holmes inquired as Miss Faith placed the remaining biscuits in a round tin.

The pretty woman set the container aside and turned to face us squarely. As she did so, her demeanour altered dramatically. There was a stern glint in her bright blue eyes and her voice took on a deeper tone.

'The devil's blaze, of course. That's what brought you here, isn't it?'

12

SIGNS AND WONDERS

Ophelia Faith invited us all to be seated at the table and Dr MacReady explained her presence.

'I knew from the school grapevine that the well-known Ophelia Faith was in fact my old friend and co-conspirator Phoebe,' she said. 'It wasn't hard to guess that your inquiries would draw you to her, Mr Holmes, seeing as she claims to have some insight into this phenomenon. I thought it would be helpful if I dropped by beforehand for a wee chat.'

'And I'm very glad you did,' said Miss Faith, her tone recovering some of its earlier sweetness. 'It was pleasant to recall those happier days.'

'And do you truly maintain, as your tracts suggest,' Holmes asked her, 'that these fiery deaths have a supernatural origin?'

'Ultimately, Mr Holmes, everything, like the universe itself, has a supernatural origin,' Ophelia Faith stated. 'When the entire world is going through a period of extreme and ultimate trial, it is only to be expected that we should witness extraordinary visitations, like the angels who were sighted over the battlefields of the Great War.'

I had heard such stories before and I recalled only too clearly the large numbers of rosaries, crosses and holy pictures to be found in the trenches in those days, by no means all of them in the possession of Roman Catholics. It was hardly surprising that, in the presence of imminent death, many sought the comforts of a faith they had probably long neglected.

'But men burned alive in the presence of friends and family,' I objected, 'surely such a horror cannot be divine in origin.'

'It is not the meek and the helpless who are being struck down,' Miss Faith asserted, 'not women and not children. It is men of influence and power, the very sort who most need to be humbled.'

'Whatever moral conclusions you may choose to draw from these disturbing events,' said Holmes, 'our task is to discover a material source so that they may be prevented in future.'

I noticed that Dr MacReady was keeping silent, leaving it to my friend to assert the primacy of science in this matter.

The lady evangelist, however, stood her ground. 'Do you recall how overwhelming the material resources of our enemies appeared to be in the darkest days of the war?' she challenged. 'And yet we prevailed. With the fall of France hundreds of thousands of our soldiers were trapped on the other side of the Channel, with doom and bloody death hanging over them. It was then that the king called for a national day of prayer for the deliverance of our men. The churches that day were overflowing and crowds filled the streets outside Westminster Abbey.'

I remembered it well. I am by no means a regular churchgoer, but on that day, when the fate of our nation hung in the balance, I too joined the throng to keep alive the flickering flame of hope. Even now I can hear the tolling of the bells across the city, the voices raised in prayer and the hymns sung with a fervour unequalled at any time since.

'The results speak for themselves, do they not?' Ophelia Faith continued. 'The German armies were held back as though by an invisible hand. A storm of extraordinary ferocity grounded their aircraft while at the same time calm waters were granted to the makeshift rescue fleet making its way across the Channel to Dunkirk.' Her eyes shone brightly as she retold the familiar and yet always astonishing story. 'Many of the soldiers trapped on the beaches told the same tale of passing through a hail of enemy bullets to find themselves unscathed, as though protected by an invisible shield. They were brought safely home in their thousands and even our prime minister, not known as a religious man, described it as a miracle.'

'It was something for which we should certainly give thanks.' I was prepared to concede that much at least.

'An ill-judged hesitation by Herr Hitler,' said Holmes, 'some unusual weather conditions and a number of lucky escapes do not lie beyond the bounds of natural explanation.'

'Really, Mr Holmes?' Ophelia Faith spoke with such assurance, she seemed to radiate an almost palpable charisma. 'Why, just the other week fire wardens in Islington witnessed a shining white figure drifting across the night sky. What else could it be but a guardian angel? If these were elements in one of your investigations, would you dismiss them as mere coincidence or would you read a deeper significance into them?'

'Madam, I am content that no part of my occupation requires me to probe the mind and intentions of the

Almighty,' Holmes answered. 'I am happy to relinquish that task to others who have a better acquaintance with His ways.'

'It is well known, Mr Holmes, that you draw the most remarkable conclusions from a footprint or some cigar ash,' Ophelia Faith insisted, 'and yet you turn blindly away from the signs and wonders that surround us in these days of crisis.'

'Can we just say that in such matters I choose to reserve my judgement?' Holmes responded mildly.

'The time for such prevarication is long past, for force of arms alone will not bring us out of the darkness.' It struck me that Miss Faith was delivering an extract from one of her sermons, but her words had about them the ring of absolute conviction. 'It will all be for nothing if at the end of our trials our country is still sunk in baseness and corruption. Our hearts must be purified if a better and cleaner land is to stand forth under God's new dawn.'

It was difficult not to be impressed by her fervour and Holmes gazed fixedly at her, as if trying to discern whether she was indeed some sort of prophet or simply an eccentric enthusiast.

Dr MacReady used the pause to intervene on a conciliatory note. 'I think there's room enough in this life for faith and science to both do their bit. And in this particular matter I should say we're all of us looking for the truth.'

I became aware of a buzz of voices and the shuffling of feet from beyond the door.

'Our prayer meeting will be starting shortly,' Miss Faith informed us. Without any trace of irony she added, 'You are very welcome to join us.'

Before we could decline, the little girl we had met earlier rushed into the kitchen, seeming flushed from more than just the work of laying out hymn books.

'Miss Faith,' she gasped, 'there's a lady come in that looks all upset, crying and everything.'

We all stood as the lady in question walked in – a thin, harried-looking woman whose greying hair was escaping in disordered locks from under her black hat. Her other garments were also black and her eyes were red from recent tears. She addressed the evangelist in a strained voice.

'Are you Ophelia Faith?'

'Why yes,' Miss Faith replied. With a gesture she shooed the little girl out of the room and stepped forward in obvious concern. 'How can I help you?'

The woman in black pulled from her handbag one of the pamphlets proclaiming the vengeful nature of the devil's blaze. 'Is it true that my husband's death was a punishment from God?'

I realised now that this was the grieving widow of Captain Roland Shore, whose dreadful end we had witnessed at first hand.

Miss Faith stretched out a comforting hand but Mrs Shore brushed it away. 'I'm not saying he was a good man,' she said in a cracked voice. 'He betrayed me many times with many women, but I always hoped . . . hoped that one day . . . one day . . .'

Overcome with emotion, she grabbed hold of the table to keep herself from collapsing. I gently placed a hand on her arm.

'Come, madam, you have been through a dreadful

ordeal, but now you are only upsetting yourself. Let me fetch you a glass of water.'

'I'll see to that,' said Ophelia Faith. She filled a tumbler from the tap and handed it to the widow.

Mrs Shore took a swallow, then, setting the drink aside, caught sight of Holmes for the first time. 'Sherlock Holmes?' she exclaimed. 'Are you Sherlock Holmes?'

He acknowledged it with only the barest inclination of his head.

The widow pulled away from me and walked towards my friend. 'And you are investigating these awful deaths?'

'I am applying my every faculty to that very case,' said Holmes.

Mrs Shore seized him by the lapels and brought her tear-stained face close to his. 'Promise me, Mr Holmes, promise me that you will find out what is happening. Can it really be the will of God?'

Though he was never comfortable with strong displays of emotion, especially from women, Holmes stood firm and took the widow's hands in his own. He spoke softly. 'I assure you, madam, that God has played no part in this, and if there's a devil behind it, he wears a human face.'

13

A DOORWAY INTO THE PAST

Once we had escorted Mrs Shore safely home and I had administered a sedative to the poor lady, Dr MacReady accompanied us back to Baker Street.

'Obviously divine intervention has got nothing to do with this,' she told us as we climbed the stairs, 'but I wanted to be sure in my own mind that wee Ophelia doesn't have any sort of connection to this gruesome business.'

'And are you satisfied?' I asked.

Dr MacReady pursed her lips. 'Well, Dr Watson, I made a point of telling her about some of my recent work so I could watch her reaction. As I was reeling off a lot of scientific talk, she glazed over as though I was havering in Swahili. You can take it from me, the lassie can barely brew a decent pot of tea, let alone concoct a chemical incendiary.'

'She is merely using these bizarre deaths to ram home her message of repentance,' Holmes concluded, 'just as she draws upon other striking events to bolster the faith of her followers.'

Once inside our apartment, we all three removed our coats and hats.

'It's funny, isn't it?' said Dr MacReady. 'Back at Lady Anne's she was just plain Phoebe Puckering, with no more religion in her than any other adolescent girl. But, as you can tell, a lot's happened to her since.'

'What exactly?' Holmes inquired as he selected a pipe from his collection.

'It's quite a story,' said Dr MacReady. 'It seems that a few years ago, after falling into bad company, she felt her life was ruined – ruined and pointless. In a fit of despair the silly lass tried to drown herself in the Thames, but luckily a passing sailor spotted her and dived in to rescue her. After getting her safely to shore, he disappeared, leaving her with the impression that he must have been an angel in disguise, sent by God to give her a new life, and a new name as well.'

'And so she became the evangelical Miss Ophelia Faith,' I mused, 'taking that first name from the drowned girl in *Hamlet*.'

'It is a curious tale, to be sure,' said Holmes, lighting his pipe.

'Interesting as all this is,' I sighed, leaning on the mantelpiece, 'we are no further forward than we were before.'

'Oh, I wouldn't be so dour as that,' said Dr MacReady. 'I've made some progress in sketching out the structure of the chemical agent causing these fires.'

'So the victims were exposed to some external catalyst,' said Holmes, his interest piqued. 'That has been my assumption all along.'

'It's not like anything I've come across before,' said the Scotswoman ruefully, 'and I've only made a start. To be honest, it might take years to work out the whole thing.'

'Still, you have cast some light on this incendiary agent?' I prompted her.

'I'll show you if you like,' she offered.

'By all means,' Holmes encouraged. He rolled out

a blackboard which he sometimes used to write down names, clues and other details of a case in order to seek inspiration from contemplating them.

We watched with interest while Dr MacReady took up a piece of chalk and began to draw an elaborate network of lines connected by symbols representing atoms and molecules. There were gaps in the design and my scientific expertise was not sufficient to make anything of it beyond the fact that it was a complex compound of several diverse elements.

Holmes scrutinised the completed drawing and tapped his lower lip with the stem of his briarwood pipe. 'Some derivative of hydrofluoric acid appears to be one of the ingredients,' he murmured.

'That's right,' Dr MacReady confirmed. 'You'll mind that it can be absorbed quickly into the skin without any immediate effect. It's been used here as a binding agent.'

'And some combination of phosphates is also present, I see,' Holmes went on. 'We must assume, of course, that the presence of this substance is not easily detected.'

'So you believe the victims were exposed to the compound without their knowledge?' I asked.

'And later, by some means I've not cracked yet,' said Dr MacReady, 'something triggered the reaction that set off the fiery effect the pair of you witnessed for yourselves.'

Holmes bit down on the stem of his pipe while he stared at the blackboard in utter absorption, as though peering into the depths of a murky pool where some lost treasure might be discerned.

'Holmes, have you spotted something?' I asked.

My question appeared to fall on deaf ears as Holmes

continued to study the board in rapt concentration. Finally he spoke.

'There is definitely something here, something naggingly familiar, and yet I cannot quite grasp it.'

'Something you've seen before?' Dr MacReady suggested.

'Perhaps, perhaps.' Holmes distractedly ran a hand over the back of his neck. 'It's as though it's hidden behind a wall at the very back of my mind.'

'Somewhere in the unconscious?' I ventured.

Holmes pressed one finger against the board, as though seeking a way through his mental block. 'It might be phrased that way.'

'Are you dabbling in psychiatry now, doctor?' the Scottish lady inquired in a half-mocking tone.

'I concern myself chiefly with ailments of the body,' I said, 'but often a patient will have problems of the mental variety as well.'

'The suggestion is a valuable one,' said Holmes with unexpected enthusiasm. 'If we are to get to the root of this case before another victim is immolated, we must use whatever methods come to hand. Watson, you are acquainted with the medical uses of hypnosis?'

'I've seen a colleague of mine demonstrate the technique a number of times,' I said. 'It has been known to aid in the treatment of pain.'

Dr MacReady frowned. 'The same trick's been used on stage to make folk cluck like chickens, or to think they're the king of Bohemia. Not what I'd call proper medical science.'

'Notwithstanding such coarse theatrical amusements,' said Holmes, 'hypnosis has, I believe, been used in the treatment of the mind.'

'It has,' I concurred. 'Hypnotic practitioners claim to have cured phobias and unlocked suppressed memories, though their results are not beyond dispute.'

'Nevertheless, I am convinced there is a vital clue stored up in here,' Holmes tapped a finger against his temple, 'and if it will not emerge of its own accord, we must go fishing for it. Could you contrive to place me in a hypnotic trance, Watson?'

'I could attempt it,' I replied, 'though I make no promises regarding the result.'

'I should have thought, Mr Holmes,' Dr MacReady objected, 'that a mind as strong as yours would resist any hypnotic spell.'

'Under normal circumstances, yes,' Holmes agreed, 'but I intend to offer no resistance.'

'If the subject is willing to submit,' I said, 'that makes all the difference in the world.'

'I am more than willing,' said Holmes. 'In fact, I insist we make the attempt.'

I was uncomfortable with the prospect of manipulating my friend's consciousness, but he was determined that we should seek out whatever memory it was that lurked in the depths of his psyche. Recalling the methods employed by my colleague Merton to induce a hypnotic trance in his patients, I fetched from the mantelpiece a silver pocket watch inscribed with a message of gratitude from a European nobleman whose daughter Holmes had rescued from the coils of a wicked and deceitful suitor. I then placed two chairs facing each other and invited Holmes to sit down opposite me.

'Dr MacReady, if you would be so good as to draw the curtains?' I requested.

She did so, plunging the room into semi-darkness, then pulled up a seat on my right to observe an experiment of which she was clearly sceptical.

'Now, Holmes, look directly at me,' I instructed.

Holmes fixed those sharp eyes upon me, but with an air of acquiescence that was far from typical of him. I held up the watch, dangled the fob from its chain between us and set it swaying from side to side. The faint chink of light permitted by the curtains flickered upon its polished surface as it swung to and fro.

I spoke now in a slow, hushed voice, as I had heard Merton do, directing my friend to empty his mind of all thoughts and enter into a state of absolute calm. I continued to speak in this fashion until his eyelids drooped then closed as he sank into a condition of complete lassitude. Setting the watch aside, I observed his absence of facial expression and the steady rhythm of his breath.

'Can you hear my voice?' I asked.

Holmes responded with a slow nod.

'Then listen to me. Somewhere in your memory there is a chemical formula or a scientific paper that bears some relevance to the case we are investigating. Go back as far as you must to find it. Imagine you are walking down a long corridor and each step takes you further into the past. Somewhere there is a door you need to open.'

Holmes nodded again. As Dr MacReady and I looked on, he turned his head fractionally from side to side, as if he were looking one way and then another in his quest. After a few moments he paused and raised his right hand.

I watched in fascination as he appeared to grasp and twist the knob of an unseen door, which he then pushed open.

'Are you there?' I pressed him. 'Are you in the place you seek?'

'Sure I am.' He astonished me by answering in a thick Irish accent. 'That's me, Patrick O'Rourke, reporting for duty,' he went on. 'I'm ready to put all my skills as an engineer at your disposal, sirs, if it will in any way aid you in spiting the English. Why, I hate them down to the very bottom of my soul, so I do, for all the wrongs they have done to my people.'

I was aware of Dr MacReady's suppressed gasp of surprise. 'During the Great War,' I informed her quietly, 'Holmes operated in the very midst of the enemy under this assumed identity of O'Rourke.'

This was a tale Holmes had kept hidden for many years and had only revealed to me a few months previously. Since she had already heard this much, I felt I had no choice but to take the lady into our confidence.

'He was a spy, then,' she murmured. 'I might have guessed as much.'

'Holmes – O'Rourke,' I addressed my friend again, 'are you there now, in Germany?'

'I am. They brought me blindfolded to this secret research facility.' Holmes's words had melted back into his own natural voice, though he spoke in a slow, abstracted fashion, as if from the far end of a long, benighted tunnel. He began to recite a variety of German names, as though greeting colleagues he was encountering in the hidden chamber of his memory.

'So much effort in keeping up the character of O'Rourke,'

he muttered. 'So many dangerous nights picking locks, penetrating secret files and blueprints. Scores of projects all directed towards the same end – slaughtering the enemy on a massive scale. I had expected to operate alone, but then . . .' There was a lengthy pause before he could bring himself to continue. 'Then there was *Hannah*.'

His voice almost cracked under the strain of an ancient grief.

Hannah Goldman! It was inevitable that in returning to that time he would speak her name. She surely was the source of the trauma that had shut off all but the barest recollection of that most tragic event of his life.

'She did not wish to be here,' Holmes said under his breath. 'She was pressed into the service of the military by threats made against her family. She was forced to work on their poisons, to devote her skills to an end she found abhorrent.' Holmes shook his head, his eyes still clenched tightly shut. 'We must destroy all this together, whatever the risk. So there was fire . . . death . . . prison . . . torture . . .'

His speech was fragmented now, his body twitching, his face a changing mask of tormented emotions as he relived those experiences he had told me of, how he and Hannah had set fire to the complex in order to destroy a new and lethal gas. They were captured and subjected to a brutal questioning that led to the death of that brilliant young woman. Holmes had escaped too late to save her and the long journey across enemy territory back to England had left him sick and broken.

'You're home now, Holmes,' I told him, still guiding him through his hypnotised recollections. 'You're home and safe.'

'In a hospital bed,' he said in a dry, cracked voice. 'They come to me, ask me to write out the formulae I memorised, to recreate the diagrams I saw. I do my best, for it is all I have brought away with me. So much I have left behind.'

These last words were a groan, and with a bowed head he fell silent.

I felt Dr MacReady clutch my sleeve. 'My God, doctor! What hell this man has been through!'

'You may gather from what he has been saying,' I told her, 'disjointed as it is, that while operating undercover among the enemy he lost someone very dear to him, someone who can never be replaced.'

For a moment the stalwart Scotswoman seemed to give way to a grief of her own. 'Aye, I know all about that. When I was just a young lass I too lost my only love in the war. I suppose that's left me free to carry on my scientific work instead of raising a covey of bairns, but I can't help wondering sometimes what that other life would have been like.'

I had not expected that she and Holmes would have so much in common beyond their interest in the sciences. They had suffered tragedies greater than my own, as Mary and I had at least been granted some years to enjoy our love before the end.

Taking a deep breath to recover my composure, I returned my attention to my friend, who was still in the grip of a hypnotic trance and oblivious of his surroundings. I addressed him in the same slow rhythmic fashion as the one in which I had begun our session. 'I am going to count to three now, and when I complete the count, you will open your eyes and return to us here in Baker Street.'

At the count of three Holmes raised his head and his eyes snapped open. It took a moment for him to recognise that he was back in his familiar apartment, and then I saw him barely restrain a shudder at the memories he had just experienced.

I was almost choked with guilt. 'Holmes, I should never have agreed to this. What I have put you through—'

He cut me off. 'Was absolutely necessary.' Jumping to his feet, he threw open the curtains and strode to the blackboard, he snatched up a piece of chalk and began rapidly to alter and fill in Dr MacReady's speculative reconstruction.

'Though I was half delirious much of the time, I was able to recall much of what I discovered in those chambers of death.' Holmes spoke with a concentrated seriousness of purpose as the chalk scraped and squeaked across the board. 'One of those secrets was a proposed formula for a new form of incendiary, a compound of chlorine trifluoride. They called it phlogiston, after the fiery element early chemists believed to exist in all combustible bodies.'

He completed his reconstruction and tossed the chalk aside as though it burned his fingers. Dr MacReady and I stared with a mixture of fascination and deep unease at what he had laid out before us.

'Now we know who brought this fiery horror to our shores,' Holmes concluded grimly. 'I did it.'

14

THE BOWMAN'S TOWER

Wherever I might have imagined our current investigation would lead us, I had not foreseen a visit to the Tower of London. And yet, the day after Holmes's painful revelation of the origin of the flaming death, here we were, crossing the stone bridge to the gateway of the famous landmark.

Down below, the moat, like so much open land across the country, had been turned into a series of allotments to augment the national food supply, and I spotted three figures hard at work with shovel and hoe among the orderly beds of potatoes, carrots and onions. It was an incongruous scene given the assertively martial nature of the stout walls and buttresses rising up above them.

We were met at the gate by a young officer of the Royal Fusiliers who escorted us through the outer defences. At the first warnings of war, the Tower had been turned from a monument back into a fortress, a stronghold against the anticipated German invasion. Artillery emplacements and fresh fortifications were clearly visible as we entered the inner courtyard, while beyond the central keep of the White Tower I could see the shattered ruins of the mint and the old hospital, which had been struck by enemy bombs during the Blitz.

This provided an ironic background to squads of German prisoners carrying out their daily exercise under the watchful eyes of their armed guards. As in days of old, the Tower of London was once more a place of imprisonment and – in the case of spies – execution.

We were taken to an office where we were greeted by an elderly man in a field marshal's uniform. This was Sir Philip Chetwode, the recently appointed Constable of the Tower, who appeared displeased at the presence of civilians in the heart of his military establishment. He was even more disgruntled to learn that we were seeking admittance to the secret government archive located beneath the Tower.

Holmes and I had been down there once before in connection with the affair of the Wright-Warrington plans, and my friend still retained the pass required to gain admittance. He presented this to the constable, who muttered a gruff acknowledgement before taking a key from his desk drawer and passing it to the lieutenant.

Accompanied by the young officer, we made our way to the north wall where he led us inside the solid, rounded mass of the Bowyer Tower, so named because in Tudor times it had housed the workshop of the longbow-maker. In 1911 an archaeological dig had discovered the original city wall of Roman Londinium running directly beneath this tower, and once the archaeologists had finished their work the government decided to expand the excavation into a series of underground tunnels and chambers to serve as a secure storehouse for a variety of confidential documents relating to national security. We entered a bare central chamber where the lieutenant fetched a crowbar from a cupboard and used it to raise up a heavy flagstone, exposing a deep shaft beneath. He switched on a light hanging to reveal a flight of stone steps that led down into the subterranean gloom.

'I'll stand here on guard,' he said, handing Holmes the key, 'until you've finished your business. You won't be long, I hope.'

'We'll be as brisk as our task allows,' Holmes assured him, heading down the stairway.

When we reached the bottom, we were faced with a heavy wooden door which Holmes unlocked. We stepped into the gloomy passage beyond, where, groping at the wall with my fingers, I pressed a switch which caused a series of bare electric bulbs to spring into life, illuminating our path.

I stifled a cough caused by the dust our entrance had stirred up and gazed at the grey walls, which were plastered with outdated duty rosters and signs cautioning against the dangers of loose gossip.

'It looks as though this place hasn't been used in years,' I commented.

'Not many people are even aware that it exists,' said Holmes. 'And yet it was here that confidential records of intelligence gathered during and immediately after the Great War were stored for many years.'

'Including the information related by you while you recovered from your arduous journey back home.'

We walked down the passage, our footsteps echoing eerily in the bare emptiness. The doors on either side of us were labelled with dates and strings of letters and numbers that described the contents of the rooms beyond in coded terms. Holmes's aspect was grave as he peered at each one in turn. We were now literally walking down a corridor into his past, and he was still visibly discomfited by the memories he had been forced to reawaken.

'I feel rather like a man who has opened Pandora's Box and loosed a terrible evil upon the world,' he murmured.

'My dear fellow, you cannot blame yourself for any of this,' I told him. 'Who knows how many lives were saved by the intelligence you brought back from Germany.'

'I suppose it is as you say,' he conceded in a flat tone.

'Besides,' I added, 'according to Dr MacReady, even the restored formula you reconstructed would prove too unstable to be employed in the precise and targeted manner required to commit these murders.'

Holmes stopped at one of the doors and peered closely at the label fixed there. 'And yet, Dr MacReady's original analysis and my recollections of phlogiston are too closely matched to be a coincidence.' He opened the door and flicked on the light. 'If I understand this filing system correctly, the answers await us here.'

The room was roughly twenty feet square. A dozen filing cabinets lined the walls, and a table and flimsy wooden chair sat in the centre. All were covered with dust and a dank smell hung in the air. Even though we were on the opposite side of the Tower from the river, I had the impression that water from the Thames was seeping through the earth to surround the catacombs.

Holmes glanced over the cabinets and quickly found the one he wanted. Pulling open a drawer, he flipped through the files with nimble fingers, finally stopping to withdraw the one he sought. Standing at his shoulder I saw that it was labelled *Phlogiston* in faded blue letters.

'So the file is still here,' I said. 'Were you expecting it to have been removed?'

Holmes whipped through the contents of the folder and sniffed. 'These are simply pages removed from a scientific journal, most of which relate to the varied uses of benzene compounds. The documents relating to phlogiston have been removed and replaced.'

I leaned forward to peer at the papers for myself. 'Removed by the authorities?'

'If it was done with authorisation, why should anyone go to the trouble of making it look as if nothing had been taken? No, some individual on his own initiative, and for his own reasons, has taken the original documents, substituting these worthless pages so that to the casual eye the folder would appear to be intact.'

'You believe, then, that whoever removed the real documents is behind these fiery assassinations?'

'It is a logical inference. But now we have a trail to follow. The heading on these pages shows that they were removed from the autumn 1938 issue of the *Journal of Chemical Studies*, so our visitor must have called after that date.'

'Is there any way to identify him?'

'The constable will have a log in which the name of anyone entering this archive is recorded. We will find our suspects there.'

There had been only ten visitors to the underground archive since 1938 and none after 1940. Holmes arranged for personnel files and other relevant records to be delivered to Baker Street, then set to work analysing their contents. Following a night in which he slept little and smoked much, I joined him to review the results of his labours. While I eagerly consumed the breakfast Mrs Hudson had prepared, Holmes took a swallow of coffee and stood by the blackboard on which he had written a list of ten names.

'Major Bennington Smyth has been stationed in India for the past year,' he said, picking up the chalk and striking the major from the list. 'Hutchinson is in a nursing home, Kittle died in a plane crash in 1941.' He scored off both of their names. 'Of the remaining seven, only these four possess sufficient scientific knowledge to have developed phlogiston into the weapon we have seen deployed with such lethal accuracy.'

He circled the four names: Royston Guscot; William Chalmers; Jacob Illesley; Alaric Price.

'And have you established any connection with the victims?' I inquired.

Holmes rolled the chalk in his palm as he pondered. 'All of these men and all four victims served in various capacities over the years, and any of their paths might have crossed at some point. As yet I see no rationale for why the dead men were particularly singled out. None of our suspects stands to gain by the demise of even one of them.'

'But surely no one would employ such an extreme method of murder without some definite aim in mind,' I said.

'You are correct,' said Holmes. 'I have a couple of clerks at Whitehall rooting about for some further information that may yet enlighten us. But in the meantime we should not stand idle while our man may be preparing to strike again. Since time is of the essence, you and I will take two names each and pay them a visit. With any luck one of them may let slip something that gives him away.'

Under Holmes's pressing gaze I made haste to finish my breakfast and prepared for an excursion. He selected Guscot and Chalmers for his personal attention, delegating Illesley and Price to me. It was a matter of some pride to me that after years of absorbing his methods, I was judged observant enough to return with a full and accurate appraisal of both men.

Armed with the information that Illesley was employed at Imperial College London, I made my way to South Kensington and inquired after him at the Department of Chemical Engineering. Here I was told that he had transferred to a campus in Wales some three months ago. It seemed unlikely that he would be able to direct these fiery attacks in London from so distant a spot, but I made a note of his location in case Holmes decided that it would be worth the journey to seek him out.

That left Alaric Price, for whom I had a private address on Goldhawk Road. Climbing the stairway to his apartment, I was struck by the thought that with Illesley more or less removed from our inquiries, there was now a one in three chance that Price was the man we sought. As I rang his doorbell it occurred to me that I should have brought my pistol in case the occasion demanded his arrest.

When the door opened I saw before me a slight, stooped figure whose gimlet eyes peered unwelcomingly at me from behind the large lenses of his spectacles. The cuffs of his striped shirt were frayed and there was a mustard stain on his waistcoat. He could hardly have cut a less menacing figure.

'I'm sorry,' he said in a high-pitched Welsh accent, 'but I have nothing to spare for any of your charitable endeavours.'

He began to close the door, granting me barely enough time to thrust out a hand to keep it open. I had no idea what it was in my bearing or attire that led him to the conclusion that I was collecting money for charity, but I felt it incumbent upon me to clarify my intentions without delay.

'My name is Dr John Watson,' I stated with the firmness of a man on official business. 'I am working with the War Office on the review and reorganisation of certain archives.'

This was the pretext Holmes and I had agreed upon, being close enough to our purpose to open a line of relevant questioning without giving away our underlying intentions.

'The War Office?' Price responded guardedly. 'I resigned my post there some considerable time ago.'

'Yes, I am aware that you now work as an independent scientific consultant for a number of private businesses,' I said, hoping to conciliate him. 'This matter is, however, of some importance and I promise not to take up more than a few minutes of your time.'

After a moment's hesitation he gave way and let me enter.

The front room was less shabby than Price's personal appearance would have led me to expect. The furnishings were few and simple: a pair of armchairs, a table and stool, and a small fireplace, on the mantel of which several framed photographs were perched. Everything looked clean and dusted. Price stood in the centre of the room with his arms folded and eyed me with an unusual curiosity.

'You've come alone?' he inquired.

'Quite alone,' I assured him. He struck me as a suspicious sort and I wished to set him at his ease. 'Do you carry on any of your work here at home?' I asked pleasantly.

'Sometimes. You may be sure that I keep my chemical supplies safely locked up.'

'Before you became a private consultant, I believe that for ten years you worked at various laboratories and military research establishments.'

'Not happily, I can assure you,' the Welshman responded.

'Were your duties so trying, then?'

'My duties, no.' Price uncrossed his arms and rubbed the flat of his hand against the side of his trousers. 'But I took no pleasure from being at the beck and call of tin-hat soldiers and officious busybodies.'

'I hope I may discount myself from either of those categories,' I said, doing my best to soften his hostility. 'I thought you might be able to tell me something about your time as a researcher for the government.'

He gave me a sour look. 'There is really nothing to tell. My researches were quite routine, being assigned by my superiors.'

'And your current researches?' I encouraged.

'Are entirely confidential,' Price answered brusquely.

'You cannot expect me to violate the confidence of my clients any more than you would yourself.'

Difficult as it was not to be provoked by his manner, I maintained a polite demeanour. 'It was not my intention to be intrusive. However, it is important that we discover what has become of certain missing documents.'

Price's eyes narrowed behind the thick lenses of his spectacles. 'If you have mislaid any documents, then you should take responsibility for your own carelessness. That is something I heard often enough.'

Suddenly, as though aware that his attitude had become overly harsh, he forced a weak, apologetic smile. 'Forgive my rudeness. I really should have offered you a drink, doctor. There may be some Madeira in the kitchen.'

Without waiting for a response, he disappeared through a door into the further part of the house. I was grateful for the opportunity to scrutinise the contents of the room unobserved, and began my examination with a thoroughness I was sure Holmes would have approved of.

15

A LONELY MAN

Spread across the table were some bills and a copy of the *London Bulletin* periodical opened to the crossword, which was partially completed. On the bookshelf I spotted some volumes of entomology such as *A Compendium of South American Beetles* and *A Biological Study of the Ant*. There were also a few paperback detective thrillers of the more garish hue, and, sitting incongruously among them, a well-thumbed copy of *The Count of Monte Cristo*.

Glancing at the door Price had disappeared through, I reflected how much I would have liked to gain access to his store of chemicals. But even if I achieved that, it was beyond my scientific knowledge to discern whether they included the ingredients for the deadly phlogiston.

Instead I moved to the mantelpiece for a closer look at the photographs, which might give me some insight into Price's personal life. All of them featured a pretty, curly-haired woman, sometimes alone, sometimes in company with Price. It seemed a safe guess that this was his wife, though there was no other sign of her presence here in his apartment.

One picture in particular caught my eye. In it the woman was seated on a blanket on the grass, waving a small triangular sandwich and smiling, presumably at Price as he took the photograph. It was reminiscent of a picture I had taken of my own dear Mary only months before her untimely death. Though my recent friendship with Miss Abigail Preston had somewhat alleviated my lasting grief, that particular memory still struck me with a pang of sadness.

'I'm afraid I was mistaken – there is no Madeira in the house.'

Startled by the voice so suddenly close at hand, I turned quickly. Price was standing only a few feet behind me and now wore a lab coat over his ordinary clothes. I tried to cover my discomfiture by pointing at the picnic photograph.

'What a very lovely picture. Your wife?'

'My late wife.' Price took a step back away from me. 'She died a few years ago.'

I nodded sympathetically. 'I myself know the pain of such a loss. I shall never cease to mourn my Mary.'

'My Gwendolyn was very dear to me. Whatever people might have thought, we were very happy together.'

As he gazed at the photograph a conflict of emotions seemed to twist his features.

'I believe no two couples are alike,' I said, encouraging him to speak further. 'Each finds its own particular form of happiness, perhaps not understood by others.'

He was clenching and unclenching his right hand and his voice took on a grating edge. 'She was an innocent, you see; almost a child, in spite of her age. It was hardly her fault that others took advantage of her easy nature.' He grimaced as though suddenly afflicted with a physical pain. Then he drew himself up and his eyes narrowed as if he believed he had said too much.

I was suddenly aware that there was an astringent scent in the air that caused a prickling sensation in my nostrils. I looked around for the source but could see none.

'What,' I asked Price, 'is that unusual odour?'

He gave an ostentatious sniff. 'I smell nothing. I do use a disinfectant around the house that I suppose I have become inured to. Perhaps that is what is causing your discomfort.'

By the time he had finished speaking, the prickling sensation had passed and I could no longer detect the distinctive smell that had struck me so forcibly only moments before.

'I expect that's it,' I agreed, in spite of not being entirely convinced. 'Anyway, it seems to have passed now.'

'Well, I'm sure you have pressing business back at Baker Street.' He gestured at his lab coat. 'And as you can see, I must get back to my own work.'

He ushered me out of the front door and I heard the lock snap behind me. I didn't know what to make of this queer little man. I had certainly seemed to touch upon a sensitive spot in reference to his wife, but whether that had any possible bearing on our investigation, I could not say.

When I returned to our apartment, I found Mrs Hudson setting out a pot of tea and a plate of scones for Holmes and Dr MacReady. Our landlady was chatting happily with her fellow Scot, but now withdrew to leave us to our discussions. I noticed that Dr MacReady had brought with her a compact cylinder with a rubber nozzle attached, which I supposed had some connection to her chemical researches.

'Well, Holmes,' I asked, 'did your interviews with Guscot and Chalmers bear any fruit?'

'None at all.' Holmes gave a dissatisfied grunt. 'Either both are innocent or one is a master of dissimulation. And you, Watson, what have you to report?'

We sat down at table and I helped myself to a scone while Dr MacReady poured us each a cup of tea. I explained about Illesley's absence then recounted what I judged to be the pertinent features of my meeting with Price. My description of his reading matter appeared to pique my friend's interest.

'Books about insects, you say?'

'Yes. I suppose entomology is a hobby with him.'

'Quite so, quite so. Do go on.'

When I had completed my report, Holmes set aside his cup and stood up. He began pacing the room, which was often his habit when he was reviewing facts and ordering them in his mind.

'According to the further information I have now received from Whitehall, Major General Talman was in charge of the army explosives factory at Sidbury during the time when Price was working there. Price was dismissed from his duties when negligence on his part led to an explosion which injured two lab technicians.'

'Presumably then it was Talman who oversaw his dismissal,' I said.

'And Dr Wallace Carew was a senior director at the government research laboratories in Wolverhampton.' Holmes continued his train of thought. 'While Price was stationed there, two projects of his were cancelled so that resources could be diverted to a project being directed by Carew.'

'You're beginning to paint a very intriguing picture,

Mr Holmes,' commented Dr MacReady. 'Was this man Price ever under Captain Shore's authority?'

'There is no direct connection as such, but what Watson has unearthed is very suggestive.'

I wasn't aware that any part of my report had shed any light on the matter. 'How do you mean, Holmes?'

'By your account,' Holmes explained, 'the late Mrs Price was a pretty woman and, according to her husband, she had a trusting nature that caused her to be led astray. From the bitterness of Price's tone, as you have described it, I think it safe to assume that she was led astray by men. And what did Captain Shore's widow make clear to us?'

'Why, that he was a womaniser!' exclaimed Dr MacReady.

'And while Sir Leopold Denby, victim number two, was not directly involved in Price's work,' said Holmes, 'they moved in the same circles and he was three times divorced on grounds of adultery.'

'What you're suggesting, Holmes,' I said, 'is that Price bore a grudge against two men who crossed him in his career . . .'

'While the other two had affairs with his wife,' Dr MacReady concluded. 'It wouldn't be the first time that's been a motive for murder.'

'So there is no political motive in any of this?' I was almost appalled to think that behind these terrible deaths there were no enemy agents, no criminal mastermind like Moriarty, only one sad and lonely little man.

'No, there is no grand scheme,' said Holmes, 'no plot to undermine the government or the war effort. Each of these killings is an act of petty revenge by a man eaten up with personal bitterness.'

'Good God, Holmes!' I exclaimed, rising to my feet. 'Something else has just struck me. When I was leaving his flat, Price said he was sure I must have pressing business at Baker Street.'

'And you had made no mention of your address?'

'I'm quite sure I had not.'

'Isn't it possible,' suggested Dr MacReady, 'that Price recognised Dr Watson's name from his published accounts of your cases, Mr Holmes? The fact that you've an apartment in Baker Street is fairly well known.'

'If that was so,' Holmes objected, 'why did he not comment upon it? Why did he not ask why Sherlock Holmes was taking an interest in his affairs?'

'I have no answer to that,' I admitted.

'Damn me for a fool!' my friend exclaimed, striking his palm forcefully against his forehead. 'Watson, kindly fetch me Wednesday's *Times*.' He waved a hand in the direction of the rack where he kept his archive of recent newspapers while his eyes gleamed and his brow furrowed in a fury of concentration.

Dr MacReady stood and peered at my friend in sincere concern. 'Mr Holmes, are you feeling all right?'

In spite of my puzzlement, I quickly fished out the edition in question and handed it to him. Laying it on the table he tapped his temple with his forefinger, as though to stimulate his thoughts.

'Don't you see, Watson? The message!'

Now I understood. 'Of course! This is the issue you

named as being the key to the coded message Moriarty challenged you to identify.'

'Exactly. But I was so insufferably pleased with my swift identification of the key, I did not stop to think there might be more to it than a mere test. Now if I can just recall the sequence of numbers.'

He closed his eyes and muttered under his breath.

'Three . . . two . . . seventeen . . . one . . .'

Still muttering, he flipped rapidly through the pages of the newspaper and loudly announced each word as he found it.

'I . . .
will . . .
find . . .
him . . .
first!'

'I will find him first?' I repeated numbly. 'Do you mean to say . . . ?'

'Yes, that Moriarty was flaunting his intent right before my eyes.' Holmes flung the newspaper aside in disgust. 'Even as he handed me that challenge, he was already directing his considerable resources into a hunt for our mysterious fire-raiser.'

'Are you saying he has identified him?'

'Yes, and recruited him. That is why Price knew all along exactly who you were. Moriarty, or more likely one of his agents, had warned him to be prepared for your visit.'

'But to what end . . . ?' I began before the words caught in my throat.

I was suddenly and horrifyingly aware that I had broken out in a hot sweat. My skin was prickling all over with a sweltering sensation, as though I were facing the direct blast of an exposed furnace. My heart gave a violent lurch as the dreadful realisation swept over me that I was about to become the latest victim of the devil's blaze.

Tiny threads of smoke began to filter through my shirt front.

'Watson!' Holmes cried out in alarm.

He stretched out a hand towards me, but as he did so, Dr MacReady's voice rang out sharply. 'Step aside, Mr Holmes!'

She had the canister in her hands with the nozzle aimed my way. As Holmes dived out of the line of fire, she gave the nozzle a twist, releasing a jet of foul-smelling chemical foam. It struck me squarely in the chest and spread.

'Turn, man, turn!' Dr MacReady ordered in a harsh Scottish burr.

I spun about while she maintained the expanding stream of froth. Within seconds the searing fever in my flesh began to subside. By the time the canister was empty, the fire had died out, leaving me drenched to the skin but alive.

The shock of my narrow escape turned me weak at the knees. As my legs folded under me, a darkness overwhelmed my senses and I dropped, insensible, to the floor.

16

MARKED FOR DEATH

As I swam groggily back into consciousness, a lingering whiff of chemicals caused me a short-lived pang of panic. That fear evaporated with the realisation that I was lying atop a spread of towels on the familiar leather sofa of our front room.

Holmes was in a chair at my side, watching me closely, his lean face pale and drawn. When he saw me awake, he leaned forward and clasped my arm. 'How are you doing, old man?'

Peering down, I saw that my waistcoat and shirt had been pulled open and a soothing salve from my own medical supplies had been rubbed into my chest and abdomen. The skin was an angry shade of red, like a bad case of sunburn, and was still smarting in spite of the ointment. Nevertheless, I was profoundly relieved to see there was no harm done that wouldn't mend in a day or two.

I became aware that Holmes was anxiously awaiting my response. 'I'm tolerably well,' I croaked, 'all things considered.'

My throat was dry and hoarse as though I had been choking on volcanic ash. I looked around for Dr MacReady to thank her for her quick-thinking intervention, but she was absent from the room.

'The good doctor is down in the kitchen with Mrs Hudson,' Holmes explained. 'Before she returns, perhaps you'd like to wash and change into some dry clothes.'

With his assistance I managed to struggle to my feet and make my way to the bathroom. After thorough ablutions I proceeded to my bedroom, then returned to the parlour in a fresh set of clothes. Holmes and Dr MacReady both greeted me with obvious relief at my restored appearance. My friend steered me firmly into an armchair and seated himself close by. Dr MacReady poured a tumbler of water from a carafe and handed it to me. Parched with thirst, I quickly drained it.

'After that you'll maybe like a wee dram,' the doctor suggested with a merry twinkle.

I saluted her with the empty glass. 'Dr MacReady, I am quite sure I owe you my life. What was in that canister of yours?'

As the doctor went to pour me a whisky, Holmes explained. 'Dr MacReady has developed a powerful chemical suppressant. It is fortunate that she brought it here to show me.'

'I'm most profoundly grateful to you,' I told the chemist as she handed me a glass of Glenlivet.

Dr MacReady took a seat and crossed her long legs. 'I've not cracked all the secrets of the phlogiston formula, but I've worked out enough to concoct a mix of chemicals that will counteract it if applied quickly enough.' She paused for a grimace. 'It was a tight piece of timing,' she said ruefully. 'In a more few seconds the incendiary reaction would have taken hold and you would have been past saving.'

'But how was the deathly substance applied?' I wondered aloud. 'Price did not so much as lay a hand on me and I felt not even the tiniest prick of a needle.'

'He's developed the original formula into a chemical

mist,' Dr MacReady explained, 'which he sprayed into the air around you. It quickly penetrated your clothing and was absorbed into your flesh.'

'He must have had some sort of dispenser in his lab coat,' I guessed, 'and concealed it before I could spot what he was up to. I remember I caught a whiff of some unpleasant odour, but it was so brief that I suspected nothing.'

'You noted his interest in entomology,' Holmes reminded me. 'It is more than likely that he took his inspiration from the insect world.'

'I'd say you've got the right of it there, Mr Holmes,' Dr MacReady concurred. 'The common bombardier beetle – or *Brachinus crepitans*, if you prefer – deploys a chemical weapon against its enemies. It secretes hydrogen peroxide and a hydroquinine in two separate sacs in its body, then mixes them at the moment of attack and scoots the whole boiling concoction from the tip of its abdomen.'

'Yes, and in a like manner the American stick insect can eject its noxious spray up to two feet from its body,' Holmes added, clearly warming to the subject. 'Many species of ant deploy a similar weaponry.'

For a moment there flashed before my eyes a ghastly vision of Price as a gigantic stalking insect in a mustard-stained waistcoat. 'Whatever the inspiration,' I said with feeling, 'it is a fiendish means of assassination.'

'We can now see that each of the victims was exposed to the phlogiston without being aware of it,' said Holmes. 'All Price had to do was release the required amount as he passed his intended target in a corridor or even in the street.'

'Some element of the compound I've not nailed down

yet keeps it inert,' said Dr MacReady, 'until it's weakened by the passage of time and the natural heat of the body. That's when the ignition takes place.'

'The time elapsing between the marking of the victim and his fiery death will depend upon the strength and quantity of the dosage,' said Holmes, 'the exterior temperature and atmospheric conditions, all interacting with the individual physiology of the victim.'

'It could take a couple of days,' Dr MacReady concluded, 'or, as in Dr Watson's case, no more than an hour or two.'

I shook my head wonderingly. 'To meet him,' I said, 'he cuts such a shabby figure you would hardly think him capable of anything so monstrous.'

'I think we can speculate,' said Holmes, 'that following the death of his wife, Price sank into that state of depression in which old wrongs come forcefully back to haunt a man. Obsession takes hold and, seeing revenge as the only cure, he sets about finding the means to accomplish it.'

'I suppose, Mr Holmes,' Dr MacReady offered, 'given that he'd worked on military research, he'd learned about the archive under the Bowyer Tower and contrived some excuse to visit it.'

'When he stumbled upon the phlogiston file, he stole those documents and spent the next few years devising his instrument of retribution,' Holmes surmised. 'Whether he was able to complete the formula and adapt it to his use through some latent genius or sheer luck hardly makes a difference.'

Dr MacReady nodded grimly. 'It might well be the case that his lust for vengeance proved to be the mother of invention.'

A thought occurred to me. 'But, Holmes, in making this attempt on my life he has exposed himself beyond any shadow of a doubt as the murderer. Whether he succeeded in destroying me or not, it would be known that he was a suspect and that I had just returned from visiting him.'

'As you say,' Holmes agreed, 'he has directly incriminated himself. And that can mean only one thing.'

Not for the first time I was struggling to keep pace with my friend's rapid processes of thought. 'Which is what exactly?'

'That Moriarty has offered him protection, of course.' Holmes leapt to his feet and stabbed the air with his finger, as though accusing the professor to his face. 'In exchange, he was, on Moriarty's instruction, to lie in wait for us, knowing that sooner or later we would find our way to that apartment. When we called upon him Price was to expose us to the phlogiston and thereby seal our doom.'

I was appalled by the realisation that Moriarty was not one but several steps ahead of us. 'I am quite sure the trap was intended for you, Holmes. You are clearly the object of Moriarty's enmity.'

'Yes, my old friend, but it was you who stepped into the trap and nearly lost your life.' Holmes's sense of guilt clearly lay heavily upon him. 'I cannot apologise enough. I should have possessed the wit to foresee what might happen.'

'Think nothing of it,' I urged, touching a hand to his arm. 'We share all dangers in common and many's the time you have put yourself at hazard for my sake. But why are we sitting here instead of pursuing Price?'

I made to rise from my chair but Holmes pressed me gently back.

'I have already telephoned Inspector Lestrade and told him we have unmasked the murderer. I advised him to descend on Price's apartment at once with a full squad of men.'

'And you did not go with them?' I was surprised that Holmes should absent himself from the chase.

'I chose to remain here until I was assured that you were entirely out of danger. That was far more important to me than haring off after a quarry that was very likely fled. I think the odds are heavily against Lestrade's being in time to capture his man.'

As if on cue, I heard a familiar tread upon the stairs and moments later Lestrade entered, beating his bowler hat against his leg in obvious frustration.

'He's hopped it, Mr Holmes. The place is as clean as a whistle – not as much as a toothbrush left behind.' He took a closer look at me and his bushy eyebrows shot up. 'Stone me, Dr Watson! What on earth's happened to you? You've turned red as a beetroot.'

'Watson was almost Price's latest victim,' Holmes explained.

'If not for Dr MacReady here, I'd be nothing more than ashes,' I added.

Lestrade directed a respectful nod at the handsome lady scientist then rubbed his lantern jaw. 'This is a rum business all right. You no sooner hit upon the killer, Mr Holmes, than he slips through our fingers like sand.'

'Not without help,' Holmes muttered through gritted teeth. 'Not without help.'

That night my body recovered from its dreadful trauma by plunging me into a long, deep sleep. It was mid-morning by the time I was awake and dressed, but fortunately Mrs Hudson had no objection to preparing me a late breakfast. The contents of the tray she brought up included a letter addressed to me and postmarked Washington DC, the handwriting leaving me in no doubt as to who was the author. Eagerly I tore open the envelope and began to read a missive which expressed sentiments of the most touching kind.

As she laid out crumpets, kippers and tea, Mrs Hudson informed me that Holmes had been out since the early hours. She then casually asked a few questions about the previous day's comings and goings. After years of being in proximity to some of the extraordinary scenes that filled the life of Sherlock Holmes, she generally let them pass without comment, but she did on occasion succumb to an all too female curiosity. Not wishing to distress our devoted housekeeper with a frank account of my near incineration, I told her I had suffered an unfortunate accident but had been saved from any serious harm by the prompt action of Dr MacReady.

With a sidelong glance at the letter in my hand, Mrs Hudson remarked, 'That Dr MacReady's a braw lass, do you not think?'

Continuing to read, I said simply, 'She has many admirable qualities, to be sure.'

She straightened her apron and assumed a posture of authority. 'If you'll take my advice, doctor, I think the two of you would make a bonny couple.'

Taken aback as I was, I did my best to respond in

a dignified manner. I tapped a finger lightly against the letter. 'Mrs Hudson, I believe you are aware that I have already formed a strong attachment to Miss Abigail Preston.'

'The American lady?' Mrs Hudson pursed her lips and tutted in an eloquent display of scepticism. 'Well, she's got spirit, I'll give her that. But, if you don't mind my saying so, she's a mite too gallus for my taste.' She suddenly turned to face the door. 'Ah, there's Mr Holmes coming now.'

I was grateful for the interruption of this unwanted romantic advice, and at the sound of Holmes bounding up the stairs I slipped the letter back into the envelope and thrust it into my pocket.

Mrs Hudson greeted Holmes as he entered the room, then cast me a final meaningful glance as she departed, leaving me to puzzle over what she could possibly mean by that strange word *gallus*.

As he hung up his coat and hat Holmes declared, 'I perceive you have received a communication from Miss Preston.' In response to my obvious surprise, he explained, 'There is always an impish sparkle about you whenever you hear from that lady.'

I glanced down. 'Also I expect you noticed the edge of the envelope protruding from my pocket.'

Without confirming or denying my suspicion, Holmes asked, 'Might I inquire as to its contents?'

'You may not,' I answered firmly, setting to my breakfast. 'And if you attempt to deduce them, you do so at the risk of imperilling our friendship.'

'Point taken, old fellow, point taken.' Holmes threw

himself down in the chair opposite me and helped himself to a crumpet. 'I'm glad to see that you appear none the worse for yesterday's harrowing experiences.'

'I'm absolutely fine, Holmes,' I assured him. 'You've been busy?'

He grinned like a huntsman in close pursuit of a fox. 'Now that I know where Moriarty has been hiding, the way is open to get back on his trail and close the net on him and his confederates.'

I couldn't help uttering a sceptical grunt. 'His position appears very secure.'

Holmes tapped his long fingers on the table. 'That is why I need further irrefutable evidence of his infamy. I have been out stirring up my informants and putting every agent to work – Wiggins, Kitteridge, even that one-time villain Garvey. I see now how the advantages supplied him by his current post explain a number of mysterious occurrences that have puzzled me over the past few years, such as the diversion of the Liverpool express and the disappearance of a mail van in Colchester. I am finally able to draw these disparate elements together into a coherent pattern.'

'I certainly wish you the best of luck,' I said, finishing off the last morsel of kipper, 'and if there's anything I can do to assist you . . .'

'I have already kept you too long from your medical duties at St Thomas's,' Holmes apologised. 'Your patients must be wondering what has become of you.'

'You're right,' I agreed. 'I have neglected my hospital rounds in favour of this business of the devil's blaze. But now that we know the identity—'

I was interrupted by the jangling of the telephone. Holmes leapt for it with such alacrity it was clear he was expecting a call from one of his informants. When he pressed the receiver to his ear, however, his face registered extreme alarm. Slamming it down, he snatched up his coat and made a dash for the door.

Over his shoulder he called, 'Watson, follow me! We must go at once!'

I jumped up and started after him, wondering at his sudden urgency. As he bounded down the stairs he scribbled in his notepad and tore the page off.

'Mrs Hudson!' he bellowed.

In response to Holmes's cry our landlady bustled out of the kitchen, wiping her hands on her apron. He thrust the note at her.

'Mrs Hudson, phone Inspector Lestrade at once and tell him to meet me at this address as soon as is humanly possible.'

As Holmes bounded out of the door Mrs Hudson shot me a mystified glance to which I replied with a shrug, 'Please do as he says, Mrs Hudson. It is evidently a matter of supreme importance.'

By the time I got outside Holmes was standing in the road, flagging down a taxi. I bundled inside after him in time to hear him give the driver a familiar address.

'Dr MacReady's laboratory, Holmes? Why are we going there in such a hurry?'

'Because she is in the most dreadful danger.' Holmes's features were rigid with apprehension. 'I only hope we're not too late!'

17

DESTINATION UNKNOWN

'Danger?' I echoed.

Holmes turned to me, his eyes flashing. 'That was Dr MacReady on the phone – in a state of acute agitation. She managed to say, "*They've come for me, Mr Holmes. Please hurry!*" Then the phone was dashed from her hand.'

'Moriarty's men, you think?'

'Undoubtedly,' Holmes concurred grimly. Leaning forward, he banged the flat of his hand sharply on the back of the cabbie's seat. 'Faster, driver, faster!' he urged. 'There's a life at stake!'

Our journey to the laboratory in Gower Place felt agonisingly slow, even though our driver pushed his speed to the limit and several times cut across the path of other vehicles, leaving car horns blaring angrily in our wake. As soon as we pulled up outside the Ramsay Building, Holmes flung a couple of notes at the cabbie and vaulted out of the taxi. Without waiting for me, he charged into the university building as swiftly as his long legs would carry him. By the time I caught up, he had sprinted the length of the corridor and burst into the laboratory. Here I found him crouched over a familiar figure who lay stretched out on the floor – but it was not Dr MacReady. It was Miss Ophelia Faith.

'Watson!' he appealed to me, indicating the swollen abrasion on the side of the lady's head.

It was clear that she had been struck a vicious blow. At my instruction Holmes fetched a bowl of water and a towel while I examined the wound and gently prised the victim's eyes open to look for signs of concussion. Once I had dabbed the wound clean, I massaged her wrists and coaxed her back into consciousness.

'Dr Watson? Mr Holmes?' She stared up at us with bleary eyes. 'Mac? Where is Mac?'

'Gone, I'm afraid.' Holmes spoke softly even though I could see he was keyed up with a desperate need for action. 'What happened here?'

Miss Faith's features twisted with the effort of trying to remember. She raised a trembling hand absently towards her wound, but I gently pressed it back down so she would not aggravate the injury.

'Tell us how you came to be here,' I suggested, hoping it might help her to start at the beginning.

'Mac,' she began, licking her dry lips, 'Mac had invited me to come and see her at work. I was in the area doing errands and decided to drop by.' She stopped for a moment, wincing at a twinge of pain. 'There was nobody on duty at the door so I just came in.'

I too had noted the absence of a porter and wondered what had become of him.

'I heard voices from down the passage and followed them here.' Ophelia Faith's words dwindled to a whisper and her eyes drooped.

'What did you see?' Holmes asked forcefully enough to bring her round again.

With a visible effort she slowly opened her eyes and continued her narrative. 'Three men had Mac surrounded and were backing her into a corner. She was keeping them at bay with a beaker she had in her upraised hand. Acid, I guessed. Enough to frighten those curs.'

Anger at the intruders seemed to fire her spirit and her voice took on a new strength. 'When they saw me one of them turned and pointed a gun at me. He told Mac to set the beaker down or he'd put a bullet in me. She told me to run away. As if I would play the coward at a time like that and bow to the will of the wicked. I walked straight at the gunman, of course. I told him I was nobody's hostage and that if he as much as laid a finger on me he'd be bringing a curse down on himself.'

I couldn't help but wonder at the woman's courage, which, I supposed, sprang from the conviction that she was under God's protection. 'What happened then?' I prompted.

'I told them that a consuming fire awaited them if they didn't abandon their evil ways,' Ophelia Faith related with satisfaction. 'But they were so far gone in their wickedness that as soon as I drew close the man who had threatened me struck me in the head with the barrel of his gun. As I fell to the floor I heard Mac beg them to leave me alone, then I lost consciousness. Mac is gone, you say?'

I nodded.

'As are all her scientific notes,' Holmes added. 'They must want her to help them develop the phlogiston into a weapon that will suit whatever dark purpose Moriarty has in mind.'

At this point Lestrade strode into the room followed by two uniformed officers. One of them was supporting the porter, who was in a woozy condition.

'We found this chap in a cupboard out there,' said the inspector, jerking a thumb at the porter. 'He was trussed up and gagged. He got our attention by kicking at the door. Here, what exactly is going on, Mr Holmes?'

'Dr MacReady has been abducted,' said Holmes, stepping to the inspector's side. 'We must move quickly if we are to have any hope of rescuing her. Please have your men take care of Miss Faith.'

Lestrade squinted at the stricken lady. 'Do you mean that's the preacher woman? Her that made the pamphlets?'

'She is a witness to the crime,' I said, transferring the care of my patient to the policemen.

'Come along, Lestrade,' Holmes urged, heading for the door. 'You have a car outside?'

'Right enough,' said Lestrade. 'Young Perkins is at the wheel. Might I ask where we're going?'

'To a place no one is allowed to talk about,' Holmes responded brusquely.

As we headed down the corridor, I heard Ophelia Faith call out after us, 'Find her, please, find her! And Godspeed, Mr Holmes!'

The journey to Hunterswood was carried out in an uncomfortable atmosphere of enforced secrecy. In spite of all that had happened, and his knowledge of Moriarty's criminal intentions, Holmes had no evidence as yet to impart to Lestrade concerning the professor's activities. It seemed unwise to make accusations against a man placed in a position of trust and authority by the government, and we felt bound still to disclose as little as possible about the code-breaking station that he headed.

Lestrade was seated up front beside Perkins and twisted round to address us. 'You're quite sure that Dr MacReady has been kidnapped and this isn't a wild goose chase?' The latter possibility brought a scowl to his face.

'We have the testimony of Miss Faith as to what happened,' I told him.

Lestrade rubbed the side of his nose doubtfully. 'She's not exactly a reliable witness, is she? To be frank, she's a bit of a fruitcake.'

'In this case,' I said, 'I believe her account to be accurate.'

'There are other factors at play here, Lestrade,' said Holmes. 'Much as it galls me, I am bound by certain strictures of secrecy that prohibit me from sharing with you much of the information in my possession. I will have to ask you to trust me.'

Lestrade uttered an affirmative grunt. 'I'm prepared to do that, Mr Holmes, seeing as how many of your hunches have paid off in the past.'

I could tell that my friend was irked to hear his painstaking deductions described as hunches, but he let it pass. For the moment all he required was Lestrade's cooperation.

'I don't suppose you could toss a few hints my way about why we're going to this place . . . what is it again? Winterswood?'

'Hunterswood,' Holmes corrected him. 'I'm sorry, Lestrade. All I can tell you is that it is officially designated as a convalescent home for wounded officers.'

'But there's more to it than that, eh?' Lestrade scowled.

'Secret War Office stuff, I suppose. And you think Price is tied in with this kidnapping and that we might find him and Dr MacReady at this Hunterswood place?'

Holmes's hooded eyes were fixed on the landscape outside. 'It's a possibility, nothing more.'

'So it turns out that that Holy Hannah with her Bible tracts had nothing to do with it all.' Lestrade gave a snort. 'It was just this bloke Price getting his own back on some Romeos who'd done the dirty on him with his wife.'

'In a couple of cases,' I said. 'The others he held responsible for setbacks in his career.'

Lestrade slipped a hand under his bowler hat to rub his balding head. 'Well, he bears a grudge all right, and that's a fact. You'd think he might have just sneaked up from behind and stoved their heads in with a poker instead of going through all this fuss and bother to torch them.'

'By using his scientific skill,' Holmes explained, 'he was demonstrating to his own satisfaction his superiority over the men who had wronged him as well as ensuring that they all died in agony and terror.'

'Moreover, the public sensation caused by their spectacular deaths will surely have flattered his ego,' I added.

'Yes. How often it is that small men have the largest egos,' Holmes mused. 'I suppose it is a form of compensation.'

Under less serious circumstances I might have made some lighthearted allusion to his own vanity, but to be fair Holmes had much to pride himself on.

'I suppose that's the place up ahead,' said Perkins.

Peering over his shoulder I saw the gate leading into the grounds of Hunterswood. A large army lorry was emerging and rumbled past us as we pulled up at the guard post. Lestrade leaned out of his window to flash his credentials at the soldiers on duty.

'Inspector Lestrade, Scotland Yard. We're here on official business.'

The soldiers looked at each other and one of them shrugged. 'I suppose it doesn't make much difference now.'

They waved us through and we drove up the road towards the manor house. I was surprised that we had been admitted with so little fuss, but as we passed through the array of wooden huts the reason for the sentries' casual attitude became clear. Some of the huts had already been boarded up while Wrens and soldiers were carrying files and equipment out of the others to be loaded on to more lorries.

Perkins parked in front of the house. When I climbed out I had to pull up short to avoid being struck by a motorcycle speeding past on its way to the main road. In the distance I heard a bull-throated sergeant bellowing at a group of his men he judged to be slacking in their removal duties.

Lestrade planted his fists on his hips and surveyed the bustling scene. 'Well, Mr Holmes, it appears we've arrived a little too late.'

'This looks like a full-scale evacuation,' I observed. 'But why, Holmes?'

'I don't know,' my friend answered. 'Perhaps Wren Garrick can provide us with some answers.'

He pointed to where Jane Garrick, our driver on our first visit to Hunterswood, was supervising a squad of her fellow Wrens in the process of carrying some boxes out of the house. We walked over and hailed her.

'Oh, hello, Mr Holmes, Dr Watson,' she responded pleasantly. 'I'm surprised to see you here.'

'Why surprised?' I inquired.

'Because the place is being shut down, of course.' She called out to one of the other Wrens. 'No, not there, Tilly! Those files go in the green van over there!'

'Shut down for what reason?' Holmes demanded.

Wren Garrick waited until the roar of a passing truck had faded away before answering. 'Reorganisation of intelligence resources is all I've been told.'

'So where is everyone going?' I asked.

'All sorts of places,' she replied. 'Some to Whitehall, some to Southampton. I believe Hunterswood is going to be turned into an army barracks or something.'

'And what about the director?' Holmes inquired. 'Is he anywhere around?'

Jane Garrick examined some documents being carried by another Wren before directing her towards the correct truck. 'Oh, he's long gone,' she responded absently.

'Where exactly has he been reassigned to?' Holmes pressed her.

'I'm afraid I can't help you there.' She smiled. 'And no, I'm not being secretive. I honestly have no idea. I don't think anybody here does.'

I saw Lestrade emerge from the front door of the house, where he had been making a quick inspection. He shook his head as he walked towards us.

'If your bird was here, Mr Holmes, he's flown the coop again,' he reported. 'No Dr MacReady either. There's not a soul left inside.'

I was beset by a gnawing concern. 'Holmes, given how secure his position was here and the resources available to him, why has Moriarty chosen to abandon Hunterswood?'

There was a grim set to Holmes's jaw as he gazed about at the hurried evacuation that was going on all around us. 'He's playing some larger game of which we have had only the haziest glimpse. That I am sure of, Watson.'

His gaze suddenly lighted upon the distant blockhouse where we had been introduced to the Velox calculating machine.

'What is to become of that building over there?' he inquired of Jane Garrick.

'V-Block? It's been locked up and orders are that nobody's to go near it.'

'That's the place, Watson,' said Holmes, the spark of the chase once more upon him. 'If there's a clue anywhere to what he's up to, that's where we'll find it.'

As he took a step towards the fortress-like structure, Wren Garrick placed a hand on his arm to detain him. 'Mr Holmes, I told you, our instructions are that no one is to go there.'

Holmes gently freed himself from her grasp. 'I am sure you are correct. However, I am not under military authority.'

'Be that as it may,' she insisted, 'I have my orders.'

'I assure you,' said Holmes, 'that I take full responsibility and you will not be blamed in any way.'

Together he and I walked towards the great building.

'She did say the place is locked up,' I reminded my friend, 'and the doors are very stout, as I recall.'

'Not to worry, Watson,' he said, patting one of his pockets. 'I have my lock-picks with me.'

Before we could take another step we were staggered by a thunderous detonation that shook the very air. The doors and windows of the solid building ahead of us blew apart in gusts of flame and smoke. Even the solid walls quaked and cracked with the force of the explosion. Holmes and I dived low as fragments of concrete, glass and metal shot through the air over our heads.

18

THE SILENT WEAPON

There were gasps of astonishment all about us as everyone turned to face the shocking spectacle. Jane Garrick cried out, 'Oh my God!'

Lestrade uttered an even more emphatic exclamation.

My ears were ringing and I needed a moment to recover myself before speaking. 'Holmes, can it have been an accident caused by the machinery's overheating?'

Holmes slowly shook his head. 'Where Professor Moriarty is concerned there are no accidents. The building was packed with explosives attached to a timer.'

'But why?' I demanded. 'When you think of the knowledge and skill invested in creating that remarkable machine . . .'

'Clearly it has served its purpose and Moriarty has no more use for it. He wanted to make sure that no one else had access to its secrets.'

A further realisation struck me. 'Why, if not for Miss Garrick's attempt to hold you back, Holmes, we might have been close enough to bear the full brunt of the explosion.'

'Exactly.' Holmes set his jaw. 'Not only was the detonation no accident, it was timed almost to perfection.'

'What on earth do you mean?'

Holmes's eyes narrowed. 'Moriarty knew we would find our way to Price's apartment, and he used that know-ledge to set a trap to which you nearly succumbed. He also reasoned that if we survived that attempt, we would swiftly make our way here to Hunterswood.'

'Are you saying that in addition to destroying the machine . . .' I could scarcely articulate the chilling conclusion.

'Yes, that explosion was calculated to kill us. Moriarty knew that I could not resist the lure of the Velox machine. Incredible as it may seem, the professor's timing was out by mere seconds, which for us proved to be the only difference between life and death.'

Upon our return to London we learned that, after a brief visit to hospital, Miss Ophelia Faith had been taken home to recover from her injury. Her description of the three intruders proved too vague to be of much help to the police.

After supper Holmes settled down to tune his violin, an exercise that always helped him clarify his thoughts.

'Moriarty has any number of gangs in his pocket,' he informed me as he plucked the strings and made minute adjustments to the pegs. 'Any one of them might have provided the men for this job.'

He seemed much affected by Dr MacReady's abduction, so much so that I had rarely seen him so solemn.

'On the hopeful side,' I said, seeking to offer some solace, 'if, as you assume, Moriarty requires Dr MacReady's scientific knowledge, he will not allow her to come to any harm.'

Holmes frowned and tightened the peg of the E string by the merest fraction. 'He certainly wants to develop the phlogiston beyond the formula developed by Price, in order to use it for his own ends. What those ends might be, I have yet to discover.'

'I am still stunned by the notion that Moriarty could predict our movements with such exactitude that he missed destroying us by the barest whisker.'

'Clearly he has adapted Professor Kilbane's technology to purposes other than simply breaking the enemy codes. He has used the machines to calculate the future movements of his enemies.'

Chilling as was the revelation that his adversary was capable of such near prophetic brilliance, there was an element of grudging admiration in Holmes's voice.

'Whatever end can he have in view?' I mused.

Satisfied at last with the tuning, Holmes tested it with a brief snatch of Delius's Violin Sonata No. 1, then laid the instrument aside.

'That continues to elude me,' he confessed, 'though I have my agents following every possible avenue in hope of picking up his trail. I think it's high time we paid a call on Sir Anthony Lloyd to learn if there are further secrets he has kept hidden from us.'

The next morning was bathed in such bright summer sunshine that even the familiar view over Baker Street made it difficult to recall the dark shadow that hung over us. We set out for Whitehall in order to confront the man who, as head of the Intelligence Inner Council, had granted Moriarty such a breadth of action that there was no telling how far his ambitions might now extend.

We had no sooner stepped outside, however, than a gaunt figure leapt from a taxi some thirty yards down the road and hurried towards us.

'Holmes, isn't that the man we met at Hunterswood?' I exclaimed.

'Yes, it is Professor Kilbane,' Holmes confirmed, 'in a condition of some distress.'

As the mathematician drew closer, I perceived that his stark, bony features were tortured with anxiety. His shoulders were hunched as though against some unseen danger.

'Mr Holmes,' he panted, 'stay a moment.'

'Professor, whatever is going on?' Holmes asked, reaching out a concerned hand. 'Can you tell me the whereabouts of Moriarty?'

'Avalon,' Kilbane gasped. 'I must warn you what he is up to.'

He reached inside his jacket pocket for something, but before he could utter another word his head snapped sideways. His whole body jerked like a marionette whose strings have been cut and he collapsed on to the pavement before Holmes or I could catch him.

Kneeling over the stricken man, I saw blood trickling from a small hole behind his left temple.

'He's been shot!' I exclaimed in astonishment. 'But there was no sound of gunfire.'

'No,' Holmes agreed sombrely, 'and that can mean but one thing. You stay here and stand guard over the professor.'

Without any further explanation, he bounded out into the street, his gaze sweeping the surrounding buildings as he attempted to pinpoint the source of the bullet. Abruptly his attention fixed on the topmost floor of a tenement on the far side of the road. He sprinted towards it and disappeared into the vestibule. It pained me not to follow him into whatever danger waited beyond, but my duty was to the wounded man.

I removed my jacket and placed it under Kilbane's head as a cushion. The professor was still breathing, but only in shallow gasps. I judged the injury to his brain to be a fatal one.

A few pedestrians had stopped at the sight of the fallen man.

'Take cover!' I warned them, not knowing if the unseen assassin would strike again, or how he had accomplished the murder of Kilbane.

One young man I judged to be fit and keen I singled out, instructing him to run and fetch a policeman. I added that an ambulance should be summoned immediately. He obeyed with alacrity and I returned my attention to the stricken scientist.

'Professor Kilbane, what did you come to tell us?' I asked, leaning in close.

He was quite insensible and beyond communication, but I recalled that he had been reaching into his pocket for something. I located it and drew it out. It was a small leather-bound notebook, and a flip through the pages showed it to be filled with numbers, letters and symbols that were entirely incomprehensible to me.

When I looked up I was relieved to see Holmes returning. He had with him a large and unusual gun with a handkerchief wrapped round the barrel to preserve it from his fingerprints. There was a cylinder attached to it and a metal lever.

'There is no further danger,' he announced to the various pedestrians who were emerging from cover. 'Now please keep your distance. This is a police matter.'

Setting the weapon down carefully on the pavement, he inquired after Professor Kilbane.

'He's past saving, I'm afraid,' I told him, 'but I found this in his pocket.'

I handed Holmes the notebook, which he examined with interest. 'Tell no one of this,' he said, slipping it into his pocket. 'It may be of vital importance that we retain possession of it.'

'Holmes, what is that extraordinary weapon?' I asked, indicating the strange gun.

He cast a rueful but appreciative eye over it. 'It is a high-powered air rifle, silent and deadly, the perfect instrument for an assassin. It is, however, capable of only a single shot and takes considerable time and effort to reset each time. That is why I moved quickly before the killer could prepare it for a second shot.'

'And what has become of him?'

'Before I could reach the upper room where he was stationed, he had abandoned his cumbersome weapon and escaped down a back stairway.'

'Did you not even catch a glimpse to establish his identity?'

'That is not difficult to deduce. The same type of gun was used in the murder of Lord Radford, which I alluded to on our first visit to Hunterswood. It is the weapon of choice of Colonel Sebastian Moran.'

A wail of sirens announced the arrival of the ambulance with a police car close behind. Lestrade climbed out of the car and watched as Kilbane was laid on a stretcher and placed inside the ambulance. As it drove off, we gave him our account of what had happened.

'The victim was Professor Roderick Kilbane,' said Holmes, 'who until recently was a senior member of the staff at Hunterswood.' He pointed across the street to an upper window. 'The shot was fired from there using this air rifle, but by the time I arrived the shooter had gone.'

Lestrade took possession of the gun. 'We'll check it for fingerprints, of course, but I don't expect we'll find any. It looks like a professional job.'

'You should accompany Professor Kilbane to the hospital,' Holmes advised. 'It's just possible he may recover consciousness long enough to give you some information.'

'Right ho, Mr Holmes,' Lestrade acknowledged. 'And what are you going to do?'

'Watson and I are on our way to the offices of the Intelligence Inner Council,' Holmes declared grimly. 'It's time we demanded some answers from Sir Anthony Lloyd.'

19

THE SHADOW OF SUSPICION

The Admiralty Arch office into which we were escorted was smaller than the meeting room of the Intelligence Inner Council, but was decorated in the same patriotic style, with flags and maps of the empire along with portraits of former kings and prime ministers. Sir Anthony Lloyd was seated at his desk making a great show of being occupied with the many papers in front of him.

He waited until we were seated before looking up, and even then he kept half an eye on the document in his hand.

'Mr Holmes, Dr Watson, I confess I am surprised to see you here. I was under the impression that the case you were investigating on our behalf was more or less concluded.'

'If that is your impression,' Holmes corrected him, 'then you are very much mistaken.'

Lloyd leaned back in his chair and laid the document out flat before him. 'Now that you have identified Alaric Price, a disgruntled former employee of the War Department, as the culprit behind these dreadful crimes, I think we can count upon Scotland Yard to pursue and apprehend him with their usual efficiency. On behalf of the council, I thank you for your service. As far as we are concerned you are free to return to whatever private investigations you are engaged upon.'

I could not help but bridle at his dismissive manner,

but a look from Holmes told me to keep my feelings in check.

'Sir Anthony, Price is still at large and remains a threat,' Holmes explained with icy calm. 'Moreover, Dr Elspeth MacReady, whom you brought into this investigation, has been abducted.'

'Abducted?' Lloyd's tone was almost mocking as he passed an eye over his papers as if in search of a specific document. 'According to my information, she has been assigned to a secret government defence project where her expertise will serve this country well.'

I could contain myself no longer. 'Assigned to a secret project? Good heavens, man! She has been dragged by force from her laboratory and may now be subject to the most brutal coercion.'

Lloyd pointedly confined his attention to Holmes. 'Did either of you witness this alleged abduction?'

'There is a witness,' I insisted. 'We have the testimony of Miss Ophelia Faith, who was present at the scene and was herself the victim of a violent assault.'

Lloyd indulged himself in a small chuckle. 'Forgive my scepticism, gentlemen, but is this not the same lady who attributed Price's crimes to the actions of Lucifer? I am surprised that you would take her seriously.'

Holmes's ire was rising but his words were restrained. 'Perhaps you will lend more credence to the death of Professor Kilbane, murdered by a sniper's bullet on our very doorstep.'

Lloyd maintained his business-like air. 'I have received a report to that effect, though I am waiting for all the facts to be assembled.'

'You will be aware, Sir Anthony, that the professor was employed at Hunterswood?' Holmes's tone was becoming steadily sharper.

'Yes, of course.'

'I take it you are also aware that Hunterswood has been shut down and its personnel dispersed. Can you explain the reason for this?'

'It's very simple, Mr Holmes. For reasons of security, the operation has been redistributed over several locations in order to render it less vulnerable to enemy attack and infiltration.'

'And the explosive destruction of the so-called V-Block?' Holmes persisted. 'Was that also a matter of security?'

Lloyd shuffled some papers on his desk and contemplated them with the casual air of a man reviewing the cricket scores. 'Naturally any machinery too large to be easily transported had to be destroyed to keep it from falling into the wrong hands.'

Holmes took a breath and changed tack. 'Since we both view the death of Professor Kilbane as a matter for investigation, it is significant that his dying words were a reference to a project code-named Avalon.'

Lloyd's posture stiffened but he let slip no other reaction.

'In order that I may pursue the professor's killers,' Holmes pressed, 'I must insist that you turn over to me any information you have regarding that particular operation.'

Lloyd locked his fingers together on the desk in front of him. 'Even if I had any idea what you were talking about, it would be a gross violation of national security for me to hand over to you files of a confidential nature.'

'If you do not,' Holmes warned, 'and choose instead to block my investigation, the consequences for the country are likely to be grave.'

'May I remind you, Mr Holmes, that you do not hold a position of any authority in the government, the military or the police.' Lloyd's attitude was now openly hostile. 'You are an independent agent and, as such, have no right to make any such demand.'

I could abide no more. 'You, sir, are being deliberately obtuse! Were you not in the service of His Majesty, I would drag you from behind that desk and make you answer for your rudeness.'

Lloyd swung an affronted gaze upon me. 'Really, doctor, I must ask you to moderate your language.'

'It appears to me, Sir Anthony,' Holmes intervened, 'that you are obstructing me either for reasons of your own or because you are the victim of some outside constraint.'

Lloyd shifted uncomfortably in his chair. 'Since you force me to it, Mr Holmes, I must make my position clear. Reports have reached me recently concerning your activities during the years nineteen thirty-five and thirty-six. You do not deny that you were out of the country during that period and have never provided any satisfactory explanation for your absence?'

'I deny nothing,' Holmes responded. 'I did not feel any explanation necessary. I am, as you say, a private citizen.'

'Much as it pains me to touch upon so distasteful a subject,' Lloyd continued, without displaying the least sign of discomfort, 'according to reliable intelligence, you spent much of that time in Germany where you were observed in the company of Wilhelm Brandenauer, Bernhardt Ziegler and Major Frederick Fuchs.'

Holmes frowned darkly. 'Unless I am much mistaken, all of those men were leading figures in the National Socialist movement.'

'Exactly!' Lloyd concluded with cold satisfaction. 'Can you perhaps explain why you were consorting with prominent members of the Nazi party at such a crucial time?'

'No explanation is necessary,' Holmes snorted. 'The entire story is a complete fabrication.'

'It has been confirmed by reliable authorities,' Lloyd asserted.

I was utterly outraged on my friend's behalf. 'By whom exactly?' I demanded.

'I am not at liberty to disclose names, doctor,' Lloyd responded coldly. 'I'm sure you understand.'

There was an edge of righteous anger in Holmes's voice now. 'I understand very well. The source of these accusations is the man you refer to as M, known to me as Professor Moriarty.'

'I can neither confirm nor deny that statement,' said Lloyd. 'But I must caution you not to spread such sensitive information beyond the walls of this room.'

'And might I caution you,' I retorted with some heat, 'not to bring such a specious allegation of treason against one of the most respected men in the country, to whom you owe more than you can ever repay.'

Lloyd slammed his hands down flat on the desk. 'My

personal feelings have no bearing on the matter. These are very serious allegations, in addition to which I now learn that a prominent scientist has been murdered while in your company and, as you put it yourself, on your very doorstep.'

Holmes drew himself up as though he had been challenged to a duel. 'You are surely not suggesting that I had a hand in Professor Kilbane's death.'

'I am not suggesting anything,' Lloyd responded. 'But these matters must be investigated. And while that investigation runs its course, all your security clearances, Mr Holmes, must of necessity be revoked.'

There followed a few moments of chilly silence, then Holmes rose to his feet. 'Sir Anthony, I see that our association is at an end. That being the case, I shall do as you advise and return to my civilian occupation as a private inquiry agent.'

I followed Holmes to the door. As we made to leave Sir Anthony raised his voice to say, 'Gentlemen, while I await a full report on these recent events, I must ask you both not to travel beyond the confines of London.'

I glanced back over my shoulder. 'Rest assured, we shall consider ourselves so confined.'

As we stepped out into the street I let my outrage boil over. 'That bureaucratic popinjay! To imply that you played any part in Kilbane's death!'

'Ironically it may be true in an indirect manner.' Holmes appeared quite unruffled. 'It is entirely possible that Moran was stationed across the street with instructions to kill me, but when he saw Kilbane approaching with information that could prove ruinous to Moriarty's plans, he altered his target accordingly.'

'Moriarty's plans!' I groaned. 'What will it take to penetrate the intent of so devious a mind?'

'Clearly the professor fears that I may be able to do so,' Holmes mused. 'That is why he is cutting me off from any legitimate source of information by fabricating this absurd slander of a past association with our enemies.'

'It has certainly proved effective,' I agreed. 'But is Lloyd simply a catspaw of Moriarty?'

'Whether he has been bribed, blackmailed or merely duped,' said Holmes, 'the result is the same. In the absence of Mycroft, there is no telling who we can trust in government circles.'

'In which case we are on our own, eh?'

'Not for the first time, Watson. But even so, we still have options.'

20

ENTER SHERRINFORD WEST

I had arranged to work an overnight shift at St Thomas's hospital, and when I returned to Baker Street in the early hours I went directly to bed without catching sight or sound of Sherlock Holmes. I rose in the late morning to find him sprawled in his chair surrounded by folders and documents, with a particularly foul smoke issuing from his briarwood pipe.

'Ah, Watson,' he greeted me. 'There is a pot of coffee over there. Do help yourself.'

I picked up the pot and found that it was completely empty. Holmes had clearly been busy.

'What is all this?' I asked, gesturing at the expansive array of paperwork.

'Requisitions,' he answered distractedly, 'travel instructions, fuel vouchers, personnel assignments – all related to Hunterswood but directed towards a part of the country far removed from Buckinghamshire.'

I gazed in wonder at the sheer volume of the documentation. 'Where did it all come from?'

'Oh, various offices around Whitehall,' he answered unconcernedly.

'But Holmes, Lloyd has debarred us from such confidential information. How were you able to get your hands on it?'

'By the simple expedient of burglary,' Holmes answered. 'There is hardly much purpose in mastering the skills of the criminal classes if I am not prepared to turn them to my own advantage.'

I was well aware that this was not the first time Holmes had employed means that lay outside the strictures of the law in order to serve the ends of justice. Given the extreme circumstances in which we found ourselves, I was not minded to remonstrate with him on this occasion.

Mrs Hudson entered, shook the coffee pot and tutted. 'Another one drained? Mr Holmes, you'll not sleep for a month.'

'Thank you, Mrs Hudson. You might perhaps make a fresh pot for Dr Watson.'

'Would you care for some porridge too, doctor?' our landlady offered as she cleared the pot and cups away.

'Yes, you should eat, Watson,' Holmes urged. 'I anticipate a busy day ahead.'

While I enjoyed a hearty breakfast, Holmes continued to examine his 'borrowed' documents, shifting from time to time to a large map of the British Isles. Eventually he broke off and joined me for coffee.

'Everything has been directed northward,' he informed me. 'Electronic equipment, building materials, catering supplies. The official destination is different in each case, but I am certain that from there the materials are forwarded to a single location.'

'That location being?' I prompted.

'Avalon. It is a code name not for a project but for a specific place. You will recall that in Arthurian myth Avalon was an island.'

'Yes, the final resting place of the legendary king and his knights,' I recalled.

Holmes rubbed his chin thoughtfully. 'Indeed, but what lies sleeping in this new Avalon? Nothing so noble as the fellowship of the Round Table, I fear.'

Further speculations on this subject were cut short by the arrival of Inspector Lestrade.

'Good day, Lestrade,' said Holmes, rising to greet him. 'Was any more information gleaned from Professor Kilbane?'

Lestrade responded with a heavy shake of his head. 'I'm sorry to say he never recovered consciousness and died within minutes of reaching the hospital.'

'It was a terrible thing to see a man cut down like that,' I commented. 'By all accounts he was a brilliant mathematician.'

'That's not the worst of it, doctor,' said Lestrade dourly. 'I have some very bad news.'

In the face of the inspector's obvious reluctance to continue, Holmes lit a pipe and waved it at him. 'Out with it, man.'

Lestrade scowled unhappily. 'Mr Holmes, instructions have been issued for you and Dr Watson to be detained on suspicion of colluding with the enemy and being directly involved in the death of Professor Kilbane.'

'Colluding with the enemy?' I burst out. 'Surely, Lestrade, you cannot credit such a vile calumny!'

The inspector squared his broad shoulders. 'If I might speak frankly, doctor, I say bollocks to that. I'll be blowed if I'm going to slap handcuffs on the two men who've solved half the crimes in London.'

'You exaggerate, of course,' said Holmes, 'but the sentiment is appreciated.'

'Where on earth can such an order have come from?' I exclaimed. 'Who could possibly have authorised it?'

'No doubt the chain of instructions is long and deliberately convoluted,' said Holmes, 'but it isn't difficult to guess the source.'

'Now, gentlemen,' said Lestrade, adopting a conspiratorial air, 'these here orders will, I assure you, take some time to reach me, me being so busy with paperwork, as you'll understand. By the time I am available to carry them out, I expect the two of you will be long gone.'

In the early years of Holmes's career there had been a certain tension between him and Lestrade on account of my friend's amateur status. With time, however, there had developed a mutual respect and I had come to recognise the inspector for the honest and hard-working policeman that he was. But never before had I so appreciated the sheer decency of the man.

'I assume,' said Holmes, 'that we shall have at least an hour's head start.'

'At the very least,' Lestrade affirmed. 'And if there's anything else I can do for you . . . ?'

'There is one thing,' said Holmes, 'if you will wait for a moment.'

He darted to his desk and scribbled a brief note. This along with a small key he placed in an envelope, which he sealed before handing it to Lestrade.

'If you would be so good as to deliver this to my brother when he returns from America, you would be doing me an enormous service.'

'I'll see to it.' Lestrade tucked the envelope into an inner pocket of his coat. 'You can be sure of that.'

'We shall not soon forget this favour,' I told the inspector as he prepared to take his leave.

'Especially since in helping us you may be stoking up some future trouble for yourself,' Holmes added.

'Oh, I can take care of myself,' said Lestrade. 'And I think I can assure you that any inquiries regarding the whereabouts of you two gentlemen will be carried out in a sluggish and slipshod manner not at all typical of Scotland Yard.'

As soon as the inspector was gone Holmes began bundling up the documents he had been studying and thrusting them into his bureau.

'Holmes, this is an alarming turn of events,' I declared. 'What are we to do now?'

'I'll tell you exactly what we're going to do, old fellow.' Holmes flashed me an energetic grin. 'Pack up your fishing rod. We're going to Scotland.'

That afternoon two gentlemen arrived at King's Cross station and settled themselves into a first class carriage on the north-bound express. One was a stooped figure in tweeds sporting a lavish set of whiskers and rejoicing in the name Sherrinford West. The other wore a pair of ill-fitting spectacles and took considerably less joy in the name Ormond Sacker. The former was a dealer in antique coins, the latter a scrap metal merchant. It was to be assumed that a common interest in metallurgy formed the basis of a friendship that saw them travelling together to Scotland, where they expected rich pickings of trout in the rivers of West Sutherland.

The foul smoke billowing from the numismatist's

pipe proved sufficient to repel any other passenger who sought to enter their compartment, so guaranteeing them a welcome privacy.

'Holmes, I believe you have served me ill in this,' I told him.

My friend barely glanced up from his study of the late Professor Kilbane's notebook. 'What do you mean by that disgruntled accusation, Watson?'

'I mean that, while the name with which you have rechristened yourself, has a certain dash to it, I am unhappily burdened with the appellation Ormond Sacker. He sounds to me like a Shakespearean buffoon who's become lost in a coal mine.'

The amused twinkle in Holmes's eye did nothing to soothe my feelings.

'I take it that your preference is for a more mundane nomenclature, such as Frederick Smith or William Jones?'

'Yes, that would be quite adequate,' I answered shortly.

He nodded. 'I will bear that in mind the next time we are in flight from the law. You must, however, admire the papers provided us by Tobias Penderghast. The so-called da Vinci of the East End may have left behind his career as an expert forger, but he is still happy to do me the odd favour in thanks for my keeping him out of prison.'

'I was not aware until now that you kept a supply of false papers in the concealed drawer of your desk.'

'There have been occasions in the past when we have required alternative identities in order to carry out our investigations,' Holmes explained, 'so it seemed prudent to be prepared for any future eventualities.'

'Well, now that we have some hours of leisure and confinement ahead of us, perhaps you would care to enlighten me as to our destination. I take it our aim is not merely to place some fresh trout on the supper table.'

'You are correct,' Holmes responded. 'We are, as the Bible puts it, become fishers of men, or to be more specific, of Professor Moriarty. There is an island called Errinsay off the west coast of Scotland. It is home to an unnamed military installation and has been designated as an experimental naval artillery range. As such it is out of bounds to all unauthorised shipping.'

Holmes paused to relight his pipe then continued. 'The curious fact is that there is no record of munitions or any other necessities being transported there. From this I conclude that Errinsay is the final destination of all those routes of supply I spoke of earlier which appear to terminate in dead ends. It is here we will find the installation that operates under the code name Avalon.'

'What on earth can have possessed Moriarty to relocate to so isolated a spot?'

'Whatever the reason,' said Holmes, 'we must reach it as quickly as possible to effect the rescue of Dr MacReady.' He added hurriedly, 'And, of course, to put a stop to whatever devilish scheme Professor Moriarty is brewing.'

Having explained this much, Holmes returned to the study of the notebook that lay in his lap.

'What is it you are finding of such interest there?' I inquired. 'It appears to me to be page upon page of intractable ciphers.'

'Not so,' said Holmes, thoughtfully stroking his false

whiskers. 'These are detailed instructions for encoding information and programming it into the Velox calculating machine.'

'That's hardly of much use now that the machine itself has been reduced to a pile of scrap,' I pointed out.

'Perhaps not, perhaps not,' Holmes murmured, 'but I wonder.'

I realised that I had lost his attention, so I left him to his studies. At the station I had purchased a copy of one of the recent novels of Mr E. Phillips Oppenheim, an author who had provided me with much pleasant distraction over the years. Removing my ill-fitting spectacles, I did my best to lose myself in his fictional adventure as we sped northward into the greatest danger of our lives.

PART THREE

REICHENBACH

21

THE HAUNTED ISLE

We stayed overnight in a guest house in Glasgow where few questions were asked of us. We then proceeded by train and local bus to the fishing village of Portshuigh where we presented ourselves in our true identities at the cottage of Geordie Munroe. As soon as he recognised us, the burly fisherman welcomed us warmly inside.

We had made his acquaintance some years before when he had been of great assistance to us in connection with the mysterious affair of the Silent Piper, that elusive phantom whose appearance traditionally presaged the death of some member of the clan McKinnon.

The interior of the cottage was rudely furnished but clean and comfortable. Mrs Munroe had decorated the front room with small figurines of farm animals and coloured pebbles and had set a vase of wild flowers in pride of place in the centre of the unvarnished dining table. An assortment of woollen pullovers and slick oilskins hung from pegs on the wall.

Soon we were seated at table and provided with two steaming bowls of a thick, flavoursome soup made from smoked fish, potatoes, onions and milk. Once we had mopped up the last of it, Munroe poured us each a glass of the local whisky with its distinctive peaty flavour. The four children, aged between five and eight, capered excitedly around their visitors before being herded together and chivvied off to bed by their rosy-cheeked mother.

After supper Holmes was still deep in conversation with Munroe when I retired to the back room where a pair of hard wooden beds had been prepared for us. When I awoke in the morning Holmes had already departed, leaving behind an explanatory note in his distinctive spidery hand.

> *My dear Watson,*
> *Have set out early with Geordie Munroe in his boat. Hope to make a useful reconnaissance of the island from a safe distance with the aid of field glasses. I judged it best to leave you here as a reserve in case anything untoward should befall us.*
> *S.H.*

I confess that I was somewhat chagrined at being left behind, but given the many hazards we faced, Holmes was probably right not to place all our eggs in one basket, especially one which could be blown out of the water by one well-aimed naval shell.

Mrs Munroe provided me with a cup of strong tea and a bowl of salted porridge for breakfast. It was very different in texture and flavour from that prepared by Mrs Hudson. This observation led me to reflect that I was gradually becoming something of a connoisseur of Scotland's national dish.

I had no sooner cleared the bowl than I was beset by all four of the Munroe children demanding a story. Without learning the truth of our identities, they had absorbed the impression that Holmes and I were some sort of adventurers in the employ of the government and had experienced many exciting encounters all across the globe. They hopped about in excited anticipation of a tale filled with headhunters, pirates and – this last was considered indispensable – poisonous snakes.

Their demands were so insistent and expressed with such zeal that I had not the heart to deny them. So it was that they sat on the floor about my feet while I treated them to an as yet unpublished tale: the Adventure of the Javanese Monkey. By omitting some of the more gruesome incidents, which had almost cost Holmes and me our lives, and adding a few colourful embellishments, I provided them with an hour of enchantment. At the conclusion of the adventure, so rapturous was their effusion of cheers and applause that, as they rushed outside to act out some favourite incidents, I felt a momentary pang of regret at having no children of my own.

Having finished the Oppenheim the previous day, I searched the small selection on the Munroes' bookshelf. Here I found a copy of Sir Walter Scott's *Rob Roy*. Given our present circumstances, I felt a warm sympathy for the plight of the legendary outlaw. Accordingly I settled myself comfortably by a window which granted me a clear view of the harbour, and began to read.

Although I could not escape a gnawing anxiety over Holmes's lengthening absence, the novel did render my vigil more endurable. Munroe's boat, the *Flauntie Lass*, hove into view just as I reached that turn in the story when Francis Osbaldistone determines to seek Rob Roy's aid in his struggle against the treacherous Rashleigh.

Placing the book back on its shelf, I hurried down to the dockside and waved a greeting. I was much relieved to spy Holmes among the three men on board, signalling back to me.

Once they had landed and disembarked, I was introduced to the third member of the crew, a grey and grizzled character referred to as Young Hamish, which left one wondering what state of senescence had by now overtaken Old Hamish. Leaving that unlikely youngster to secure the boat, Holmes, Munroe and I seated ourselves on some empty herring crates. Pipes were lit and the captain passed around a flask of the locally distilled whisky.

'I'm certainly glad to see you returned safely,' I said, once my tongue had recovered from the numbing effect of the spirit. 'You had no direct encounter with the professor, I take it.'

'Several shells were fired into the water while we made our remote observation of the island,' said Holmes, 'and although they were not aimed in our direction, they were clearly intended as a warning to keep our distance.'

'Errinsay has aye had an evil reputation,' growled Munroe. 'Folk say that witches have used it as a site for their unholy rituals and that many a sailor has been lured to his doom on its cursed rocks.'

'I doubt Moriarty has done anything to enhance its reputation,' I commented in an undertone.

'And yet the locals did land there from time to time,' said Holmes, 'in the years before it became a military installation. In fact it has been a popular haunt of smugglers dodging the hated excise men. Based on his own visits there, Geordie was able to assist me in making a sketch map of the island, no other maps being available.'

'I've had the sea in view for some time,' I said, 'and have seen no sign of Royal Navy activity.'

Munroe rubbed his tawny beard. 'It's like I told Mr Holmes, the queer thing is that ye never see a Navy ship land there, only civilian supply boats.'

'Yes, as you said, transferring cargo from that hidden bay down the coast directly to the island,' Holmes expanded for my benefit.

'Avoiding the harbour for the sake of secrecy,' I guessed.

'Which serves to confirm that this is where Moriarty has established his base of operations,' said Holmes, 'one even further removed from scrutiny than Hunterswood. On the north side of the island, the ruined fortress of the notorious sea reaver Donald o' the Dirk has been partially restored and several new structures erected around it. Most of the coast is inaccessible due to jagged rocks and treacherous sandbanks.'

'And yet you intend that we should land there,' I surmised resignedly.

There was a bold glint in Holmes's eye. 'Yes. Tonight.'

We set out at twilight cheered on only by the mournful cries of those few gulls not already returned to their nests. I was uneasily conscious that the chugging of the *Flauntie Lass*'s engine, the creak of the deck beneath our feet and even the slosh of our keel cutting through the water were already loud enough to reach the ears of Moriarty and his lackeys. Holmes and I were done up as seamen in black caps, rough pullovers, oilskin trousers and stout rubber boots. Beneath my own pullover I had my old army pistol thrust into my belt.

There was little conversation among us, the most persistent noise being that of Young Hamish clearing his throat and spitting into the sea. Munroe cut the engine as darkness fell and we spied on the horizon a small white light that marked our sinister destination. Above us was the merest sliver of a moon, mostly obscured by a covering of cloud. Munroe and Young Hamish hauled on the rope which was dragging a small dinghy along behind us, and drew it in close.

'That warning light is set on top of the north tower of the old fortress,' said the captain as we clambered down into the little boat. 'Using that as your guide, you can make your way to the shingle just below the red cliff.'

We sat ourselves down and Holmes cast us off. 'Thanks for all your help, Geordie,' he said as we each took a paddle.

'The best of luck to you, Mr Holmes, Dr Watson. You'll be needing it, sure enough.'

Young Hamish made a low throaty noise that I took as an expression of his good wishes.

With slow strokes of the paddles so as to make as little splash as possible we made our way towards Errinsay. Holmes had learned much of the layout and history of the island from Munroe and I could only pray that this knowledge would serve us well in whatever plan he had in mind.

'Now, Watson, it is vitally important that we stay close together and not become separated once we reach the shore,' he reminded me. 'If we should encounter a sentry, remember that we are a pair of Irish fishermen whose boat was wrecked on some nearby rocks.'

'But surely even the most ignorant of watchmen will see through such a flimsy story,' I objected.

'It may suffice to throw them off guard long enough for us to overpower them,' said Holmes.

'I do wish you'd share with me whatever scheme you have in mind,' I complained. 'I feel myself to be in the dark in every way.'

'Should you fall into Moriarty's hands,' said Holmes, 'ignorance will be your best protection.'

'And should you be the one captured?' I asked.

'In that case you must get back to the dinghy and return to the mainland. Hide out with the Munroes until you feel it is safe.'

'Holmes, do you expect me to abandon you to your fate?'

I could not see in the dark, but I had the impression that he was smiling. 'Don't worry about me, old friend. In those stories of yours you've depicted me as quite the resourceful fellow.'

I could not escape the uncomfortable feeling that he was trusting to luck much more than was his habit. He had always decried strong emotions as an impediment to rational thought, but it was clear to me now, though he would never admit it, that he was being impelled onward by his deep concern for Dr MacReady's welfare. This sentiment, noble as it was, had overruled his more logical faculties and driven him to take a gamble that put both our lives at risk. I was not minded to argue with him, however, as friendship and honour demanded that I follow him into whatever hazards awaited us in Moriarty's cursed lair.

In cautious silence we neared the dark mass of the island, directing our course to the left, away from the lighted tower. Soon I could hear the lapping of the tide on the pebbly beach. We jumped out into a foot of water and clambered on to the shore, hauling the dinghy up behind us.

Crouching low, we clawed our way up a steep embankment of dry, sandy grass. When we reached the top Holmes glanced around at the black misshapen outlines of rocks, bushes and stunted trees.

'Between us and the fort lie a number of outbuildings,' he informed me in a whisper. 'I believe Dr MacReady will be held in one of them.'

Before he could outline his course of action I heard a bang and a flare exploded glaringly in the skies above us. Two more flares went off, bleakly illuminating the barren landscape about us. As my eyes recovered from the flash I saw men with rifles closing in on us from all sides.

'Well, well, Holmes and Watson at last!' crowed the harsh voice of Colonel Sebastian Moran. 'Caught like rabbits in a snare.'

Reflexively I reached for my pistol, but Holmes caught hold of my wrist to restrain me from such rashness. We were quickly taken in hand and thoroughly searched. The few items we had on our persons were taken and Moran treated my gun to a disdainful examination.

'Bit of an antique, isn't it?' he sneered. 'Same as you two, I suppose.'

He passed the weapon to one of his men for safekeeping and lit a small black cigarillo. Turning to a corporal, he said, 'See that their boat down there is taken care of and anything found aboard brought to me. Then call off the rest of the men. We have what we want right here.'

With that we were prodded roughly along a stony track towards the black bulk of the ancient fortress, where I could only imagine some terrible doom awaited us.

22

THE KEY TO THE WORLD

We were taken through an arched gateway across the dirt courtyard and into the keep. Here we were led downstairs and thrust into a cell.

'Make yourselves at home,' said Moran, slamming and locking the door behind us. 'I expect the professor will want a word with you in the morning.'

Our quarters were less grim than I would have expected. The windowless walls were bare and no shade softened the overhead bulb, but the room was furnished with two comfortable-looking cots and on the table between them was a decanter of brandy and a box of cigars.

Rather than taking any comfort from these small luxuries, I was incensed at the sight of them. 'The gall of the man! To mock us by treating us like guests rather than prisoners, and most likely condemned men at that. I'd prefer the honest brutality of being manacled in a dungeon.'

'I'm afraid, Watson, we are compelled to indulge the professor's little game.' Holmes poured himself a brandy and took an appreciative sip. 'This is his way of demonstrating that he foresaw our arrival all along and has anticipated every move we can possibly make.'

'Well, if that's the case, Holmes,' I exclaimed, 'what on earth are we doing here? The situation appears quite hopeless.'

'Don't lose heart, my friend,' Holmes encouraged. He added softly, in case there might be a listener at the door, 'He may not have anticipated everything.' He flipped open the box and turned it towards me. 'Cigar?'

I slept little that night. Even at the height of the Blitz I was able to snatch a few periods of deep slumber between intakes of patients caught in the relentless bombing. This night, however, proved to be the longest of my life. Here we were, prisoners of the most evil genius on the face of the Earth, locked in a fortress guarded by Moran's ruthless thugs. The only people who knew our whereabouts were Geordie Munroe and Young Hamish, and should they attempt a rescue they would most likely be cut down by gunfire the instant their feet touched the beach.

When I did doze off I was haunted by a persistent dream of my dear Mary waiting for me at the bottom of a long garden path, her arms outstretched in greeting. And yet, much as I had longed for a reunion, did I wish for it now? Had I not found a fresh love to live for, just as Moriarty prepared to dispose of Holmes and myself like a pair of bothersome insects then carry his criminal schemes to their wicked conclusion?

The creak of the door woke me and I saw that Holmes was already standing, awake and alert, ready to greet our host as he stepped into the room. I swung myself off the bed and straightened my clothing, then turned to face Professor Moriarty.

He was dressed in a dapper suit and was as immaculately groomed as he had been at Hunterswood. He was accompanied by two men in the uniform of Moran's Special Action Brigade, both of whom had guns trained on us.

'I hope you have spent a comfortable night, gentlemen,' said Moriarty. 'I would not wish to be accused of neglecting my guests.'

'You stand accused of many things, professor,' Holmes responded conversationally, 'but lack of hospitality is not one of them.'

'You are a murderer, a kidnapper and a blackguard of the first order,' I told our host. 'So I hope you don't expect these meagre comforts to in any way alter our low opinion of you.'

'Your opinion is of no interest to me, doctor,' Moriarty responded, 'but I hope Mr Holmes appreciates that I have treated him with the respect due a determined and occasionally clever adversary.'

'Now that I am your prisoner, professor,' Holmes gestured at our surroundings, 'I suppose I have sunk somewhat in your estimation.'

'This, I'm afraid, is the inevitable outcome of setting yourself against me in defiance of my warnings,' said Moriarty, with the air of a judge preparing to pass sentence. 'And so, Mr Holmes, it has come to this at last. After so many adventures, so many daring escapes chronicled by your Boswell here, capturing you was no more difficult than placing a piece of cheese in a mousetrap. I don't suppose you have even the least inkling of what I have created on this barren island.'

'On the contrary, I know exactly what you have been working on,' Holmes stated confidently.

Moriarty raised an eyebrow. 'Indeed? Perhaps you would care to enlighten me as to this, your final deduction.'

'It is quite obvious that while diverting attention to your activities at Hunterswood, you have been preparing an advanced chemical laboratory here on Errinsay.' Holmes spoke, as I had heard him do on so many occasions, with the authority of a man in full possession of all the facts in the case.

'Having gathered under your wing a band of brilliant but not always scrupulous scientists, to whose number you have lately added Mr Alaric Price and Dr MacReady, you have been developing a deadly gas which can be distributed from the air over a target of any size so that the populations of entire cities can be exterminated while leaving buildings and industrial resources intact. You intend to use this vile poison to make yourself a decisive player in the war, allying yourself to whichever side promises you the greater rewards.'

There was a short, incredulous pause, then Moriarty let out a harsh, staccato laugh, like the cawing of a crow. Recovering his composure, he addressed himself to Sherlock Holmes in a manner of utter condescension.

'I see, Mr Holmes, that I have overestimated you all along. You are so wide of the mark that I am almost tempted to leave you to wallow in your empty delusions.'

Holmes shook his head. 'It's too late to try to trick me now, professor. I have deduced all of your plans and have left a full warning back in London.'

'A warning?' Moriarty laughed again. 'About poison gas? It's almost too delicious.' He turned towards the door and gestured to us to follow. 'Come, Holmes, let me show you wonders that have entirely escaped your narrow comprehension.'

Under the watchful gaze of our guards, we followed the professor up and down stairways and through winding passages until we came to a heavy oak door reinforced with bands of iron. From his pocket he drew a ring of keys with which he opened the three locks barring our progress. Beyond lay a further door of solid steel, like the entrance to a bank vault. Our guards held us back and Moriarty deliberately blocked our view so that we could not see his actions as he spun the combination dial back and forth until there came the loud click of bolts sliding back.

The professor heaved open the door and beckoned to us to precede him. We found ourselves in a spacious room facing a large plate glass window. The glass was many inches thick and covered in a steel mesh to render it unbreakable. On a table below the window was an electronic device attached to a keyboard such as you might find on a typewriter, but with a number of additional keys.

'That further chamber you see there,' said Moriarty, indicating the window, 'is completely and impregnably sealed. Inside you may behold the wonder of the age.'

Through the glass we stared at the most extraordinary machine I had ever beheld. It filled the vast chamber beyond and consisted of innumerable arrays of spinning rotors, rolls of tape revolving at dizzying speed on metal wheels, and row upon row of lights flashing white, green and red. The hum and clatter of its activity was equivalent to that of a huge industrial factory, and if not for the buffering of the thick glass the volume of it would have been deafening. Compared to this monster of circuits and metal, the Velox machine at Hunterswood was a child's toy.

Our obvious astonishment clearly gratified the professor's vanity.

'Behold, Mr Holmes, an automatic calculating machine operating at speeds exceeding the imagination of any mind but my own.' He paused to glory in the spectacle before us. 'Kilbane had only the crudest notion of what he had begun. It took my breakthroughs in the field of transintegral mathematics to harness the full potential of machine intelligence.'

Holmes's eyes were fixed on the gigantic calculator, fascinated by its almost hypnotic actions. 'Might I ask what name you have given to this colossus of yours?'

'There is only one name I can apply to it, Mr Holmes,' Moriarty answered with almost breathless satisfaction. 'I call it God.'

I was so stunned by the shocking blasphemy of those words that I began to wonder for the first time if our enemy might actually be insane.

'I suppose the Velox was engaged in encoding information which could then be programmed into this more advanced machine,' said Holmes. 'And you have used the keyboard here to give it instructions.'

'Correct, Mr Holmes. It serves my will and acts as an extension of my own intellect.'

There was an almost schoolboy smugness about Moriarty now. It was clear to me that Holmes's presence here had been engineered as a necessary sop to his vanity, for this was the one man capable of appreciating the extent of his achievement.

'But you have not gone to all this trouble without a specific aim in mind,' Holmes surmised.

'My aim,' said Moriarty, 'is what it has always been – power. Soon that power shall be mine in terms that are both absolute and unassailable.'

'It is an ignoble end,' I interjected, 'and an illusory one. It will not be achieved by any amount of electronic calculation.'

'You think not, doctor? Reality itself, as any competent thinker will tell you, is made up of mathematics. The secrets of the universe, the very nature of matter and energy, are surrendering to strings of formulae on a path that will one day lead to an absolute understanding of the cosmos.'

'There are some who would claim that even the methods of science have their limitations,' Holmes objected, 'and that there are boundaries to human knowledge.'

'Idiocy!' Moriarty retorted. 'There is nothing that cannot be unlocked by the power of calculation. All that is required is a thinking machine of sufficient power, and that is what I have created. I have programmed it with one overriding command, a command that cannot be halted, diverted or superseded.'

'You are not the first to lust after such power,' I said, 'and in the end their ambitions came to dust.'

'The men you speak of blundered blindly through history without any understanding of the forces in play.' Moriarty waved a hand dismissively. 'Hence Alexander's untimely death, Caesar's assassination, Napoleon's defeat and exile. I anticipate that Herr Hitler's ambitions will meet a similar end. I, however, will be armed with a weapon all of them lacked.'

'I admit that I am intrigued, professor,' said Holmes. 'Do please continue.'

It was my impression that Moriarty was now so intoxicated with his own brilliance that it would be impossible to restrain him from bragging about it.

'If you have studied my published work closely, Mr Holmes,' he pronounced didactically, 'you will be aware of my stated belief that every aspect of human affairs can be reduced to a mathematical formula.'

'A view which has been the cause of some controversy,' said Holmes.

'Only among those who lack the mental capacity to comprehend my meaning. I have now put that theory into practice, applying it to the vast amounts of data gathered for me at Hunterswood which are now stored within the machine you see before you.'

He stared through the glass as though seeing a vision of his own destiny. 'My God machine is mere hours from providing me with an algorithm that will grant me the power to predict with absolute certainty the outcome of all future events, political, military and financial. And with that knowledge will come the power to control those events, to redirect them in accordance with my ambitions.'

'Impossible!' I exclaimed.

'Impossible, Dr Watson?' Moriarty mocked me. 'The answer will shortly be transmitted to a secure chamber adjoining my study, the ultimate predictive algorithm. Then I shall hold in my hands the key to the world!'

My mind reeled at the prospect. Was it really possible to devise a formula that would predict the outcome of every future event and in doing so allow Moriarty to seize control of history itself?

'I must congratulate you, professor,' said Holmes, 'for you have truly outdone yourself. You stand now upon a peak of vanity and ambition so exalted that your fall will be terrible indeed.'

'There will be no fall for me, Holmes.' Moriarty's words were edged with pure malice. 'But as for you, I believe it is time to put an end to your troublesome existence once and for all.'

23

THE DEAD MAN'S POOL

We were taken under guard to Professor Moriarty's study, where Colonel Sebastian Moran waited. Here we could see the steel door which barred the way into the room where a teleprinter would in due course reveal the result of the machine's monstrous cogitation. On the opposite wall, in stark contrast to the abstract works which had decorated his Hunterswood office, hung a painting of the professor himself executed in a style reminiscent of those famous portraits of Napoleon with which we are all familiar.

Moriarty seated himself behind the desk and observed with some gratification that Holmes had paused before the portrait.

'It is a tolerable likeness,' my friend noted, 'but the technique lacks Birley's usual finesse. I suspect his heart was not in this project, no matter how well he was rewarded.'

Oswald Birley was an artist of some renown, and well known for his portraits of members of the royal family. I could only think that he had been compelled to serve the ego of Professor Moriarty under some form of duress.

'I have not brought you here to serve as an art critic,' Moriarty retorted with asperity, 'but to demonstrate to you exactly how futile have been your efforts to frustrate my designs.'

The guards nudged us back with the muzzles of their rifles to keep us at a safe distance from their master. Moran stood at the professor's side with one hand resting menacingly on the butt of his holstered pistol.

'I really must compliment you, professor, on your remarkable achievement,' said Holmes. 'You have made the most inventive use of the blind trust placed in you by His Majesty's government.'

'In the early days of the war, as you will recall,' said Moriarty, happy to boast of his achievements, 'things looked so dark that those timid men were happy to grant me every authority and every resource so that I might help them survive a crisis that threatened to destroy this country and its far-flung empire. That I have suborned those advantages to my own ends I count as payment for the service I have rendered in turning the tide of the war.'

Holmes glanced at the steel door beyond which the Moriarty's diabolical scheme would soon be bearing fruit. 'I must warn you,' he said, 'that none of this will keep you from an inevitable reckoning with justice.'

'What you call justice, Holmes, is merely custom,' scoffed the professor, 'custom which varies from tribe to tribe and from age to age. It carries no weight with me, I assure you. I recognise no authority outside of my own will.'

I was wondering at the vastness of the man's ego when Alaric Price was ushered into the office, with Dr MacReady close behind.

'Ah, my other guests,' Moriarty announced, rising to his feet.

'Dr MacReady, you are unharmed?' Holmes asked

the question with more earnest concern than he was accustomed to display.

'Och, I've been locked away in a lab with this wee chappie here,' the chemist indicated Price with a disparaging tilt of the head, 'but I've suffered worse.'

'While your guesswork as to my aims was depressingly mundane, Mr Holmes,' said Moriarty, 'I do foresee possibilities in this interesting chemical, for the existence of which I believe you bear some responsibility.'

He reached into his pocket and drew out a small vial of vivid emerald fluid. He held it up to the light so that it filled with a lurid glow. 'So little of it left,' he mused. 'But with two skilled scientists given every incentive to exercise their talents, I believe more can be produced and its function expanded.'

'The difficulties of stabilising the compound remain,' Price stated sullenly. 'Your incessant demands will not remove them.'

'But as you can see, I have made prisoners of the men who would bring you to justice,' Moriarty informed him. 'And so long as you continue the work I have assigned you, you will remain beyond the reach of the authorities. That being the case, I would advise you to keep yourself well within the bounds of my favour.'

Brandishing the vial before him, he addressed himself to Holmes. 'Once I have my map of the future, Mr Holmes, this weapon will give me the power to divert history's course along any path I choose.'

'It will allow you to carry out a few spectacular assassinations, to be sure,' Holmes conceded, 'but that will hardly grant you the sort of power you so fervently dream of.'

'You think not?' Moriarty shook his head in indulgent condescension. 'You may or not be aware, Mr Holmes, that a number of experiments have been carried out to assess the effect of an external radiation on various chemical reactions. What I have in mind is an advanced form of phlogiston, one which remains dormant until activated by a particular radio frequency.'

He gazed at the vial in his hand as though staring into the depths of some satanic crystal ball. 'Imagine a whole population doused in phlogiston, knowing that with the flick of a switch they can be incinerated by means of a radio signal. They would be the most obedient of servants.'

I had rarely witnessed Holmes regard another human being with such naked disgust. 'Let us be blunt, professor. They would be slaves.'

'Yes. How delicious!' Moriarty pursed his lips as though savouring the sweetness of a fine liqueur. As he slipped the vial back in his pocket Price took an aggressive step towards the desk.

'You think very highly of yourself, Moriarty,' the Welshman spat, 'but at root you're just like all the rest, a strutting, self-important tyrant, using me for his own ends.'

'Have a care, Mr Price,' the professor admonished. 'While I value your services, my patience has its limits.'

With the suddenness of a striking cobra Price pulled from his pocket a sharpened shard of metal and with a wordless screech of rage threw himself at the professor.

Moriarty recoiled violently, almost upsetting his chair. In the same instant Moran pulled out his pistol and fired three rapid shots. Price sprawled across the desk, the crude weapon dropping from his limp fingers. For a moment the whole room was frozen in stunned silence like a wax tableau. Then Sherlock Holmes spoke.

'I take it, professor, this is an eventuality you did not foresee.'

Moriarty was white with shock and rage. 'The fool,' he grated, 'the stupid, senseless fool! Why would he do this?'

'He was a small man,' I said, 'but he nursed a great hatred for anyone in authority over him.'

'Or anyone who took advantage of him,' added Holmes. 'Your mistake, professor, was to cast yourself in that exact role. Very ill-considered of you, I must say.'

No one hindered me from making a quick inspection to confirm that the little chemist was indeed dead. Moran summoned two soldiers to carry the corpse away. Moriarty eyed the bloodstains on the desk before him, then turned a malicious gaze upon Holmes.

'This might almost be a preview of your own fate, Mr Holmes. Now that I have demonstrated to you the utter futility of all your endeavours, there is no further satisfaction to be gained from your continued existence.'

Dr MacReady took a tentative step towards my friend but a soldier seized her arm and held her back. She took a deep breath and made a dignified appeal to Moriarty.

'Please, professor, spare Mr Holmes, and I promise I will do whatever you ask, even if it means delivering to you a weapon of the most hateful kind.'

'Spare Sherlock Holmes?' Moriarty rebuffed her plea with a sneer. 'No, no. He is far too dangerous to keep alive and I am not so reckless as to take such a chance. No, you must die, Mr Holmes. But what is it to be? The bullet? The knife? The garrotte perhaps?'

Dr MacReady and I exchanged despairing glances, aware that we were now no more than spectators witnessing this climactic conflict between two implacable foes.

'Really, professor, you disappoint me,' said Holmes. He seemed entirely composed and casually took a cigarette from the box on Moriarty's desk. 'You preen yourself on your supposed genius, but now, when it comes to disposing of your greatest enemy, you reveal yourself to be no more than a common thug. Bullets indeed! Knives!'

He lit his cigarette and took a long draw.

Moriarty seethed under the heat of his adversary's disdain.

'I suppose you can devise a more fitting end to your existence?' he challenged spitefully.

'Allow me a moment of thought,' said Holmes. He blew out a thin ribbon of smoke and watched it rise to the ceiling with a contemplative air.

Moriarty's pique passed and he gave a mocking shake of the head as he tolerated Holmes's silent pondering. It was, however, only a few moments before my friend spoke again.

'A previous denizen of this castle was, I believe, a seagoing brigand who rejoiced in the bloodthirsty name Donald o' the Dirk. You have heard of him, professor?'

'Of course. I am aware of the island's history.'

'Then you will recall,' Holmes continued smoothly, 'that he had a unique method of disposing of those prisoners whose lives were nothing to him but a source of entertainment.'

'I have heard a tale of some sort. He drowned them, did he not?'

'You put it too baldly. There is a cove surrounded by rocks on the western side of the island which has a crag in the middle of it. It is referred to by the locals as Dead Man's Pool.'

'I'm sure you find this local folklore fascinating, Mr Holmes,' Moriarty snapped impatiently, 'but do please get to the point.'

Holmes stubbed out his cigarette in a nearby ashtray. 'The point is, professor, that Donald had a pair of iron rings fixed to the crag. The victim was wrapped in a chain which was then wound through the rings and fastened with padlocks. There was no possible means of escape and the victim could only watch helplessly while the water rose inch by fateful inch until, at high tide, he was completely submerged and, of course, horribly drowned. I submit that, were our positions reversed, that is the method I would employ to put a final end to you.'

I was appalled that Holmes should make such a proposal. Surely a quick end was preferable to this drawn-out torture. Moriarty, however, was clearly intrigued by the prospect of destroying his enemy by a method that involved such extended suffering. He stood up, walked behind his chair and leaned upon it. Regarding Holmes with a cold smirk, he wagged a finger at him.

'Ah, Holmes, you poor fool, I understand exactly what you're doing. You have been reduced to that most pitiable gambit of all – you're playing for time. Well, whether hours or only minutes remain to you, I can assure you with absolute certitude that no help is coming.'

To my dismay I discerned the slightest weakening of my friend's resolve, a slackening in the firmness of his jaw and a dimming of the steely glint in his eyes. Worse still, I was quite sure Moriarty observed it too.

'So, Professor Moriarty, what is your decision?' Holmes asked.

A cruel smile touched the professor's lips and his head swayed from side to side in a repellent, almost reptilian fashion.

'Yes, let it be as you suggest.' He flipped open his pocket watch. 'It will be high tide in precisely ninety-four minutes. More than enough time to fetch a length of chain and carry out this ingenious proposal.'

The blood in my veins turned to ice at the pronouncement of the death sentence.

Moriarty snapped the watch shut and pocketed it. 'As the minutes tick by and the waters rise, that minuscule scintilla of hope to which you yet cling will be extinguished, along with your life.'

Shaking off the grip of her guard, Dr MacReady pushed forward and planted her hands on the desk. 'If he is to die, you may as well kill me too,' she stated firmly, 'because you'll get no help from me in your foul plans.'

'Oh, I think Dr Watson will make a perfectly adequate hostage for your good behaviour,' said Moriarty coolly before turning back to Sherlock Holmes. 'I grant you this one meagre consolation, Holmes: while I hold myself your intellectual superior in every department, in the matter of your own demise I bow to your superior invention. I shall be sure to include it as an amusing footnote in my memoirs.'

A pair of soldiers escorted Dr MacReady back to her laboratory while Holmes and I were led at gunpoint out of the fortress, with Moriarty gloating over us every step of the way.

It was a long, miserable walk to the place of execution, but in the course of it Holmes appeared to recover his strength of spirit. His head was nobly upraised and his bearing was every inch that of a man undaunted by the inexorable doom that lay before him. We came to the curving edge of a grey, weather-worn cliff that surrounded a circular pool and I stared down gloomily at the hungry waves below.

I wished desperately for some words of comfort or encouragement to offer my friend, but as I stared down at the gaunt rock rising out of the lapping waters, my heart sank and I was robbed of speech. It was as if a merciless fate had placed it here to serve as a gruesome instrument of death.

Clearly visible were the two iron rings, rusted but plainly sound, fixed to metal spikes that were driven deep into the rock. I could only imagine the sufferings of the many men – and, for all I knew, women too – who had struggled in vain against their unyielding bonds while the cold waters of death welled up to obliterate their unhappy existence.

Gripped firmly between a pair of guards, I was compelled to watch helplessly as Moran and two of his men marched Holmes down a steep path and into water which was already waist-deep. Moriarty watched with ghoulish glee as they wound the length of chain around Holmes's body, pinning his arms to his side. They then ran the ends of the chain through the rings, pulling each end tight and fastening them with a padlock that was far beyond his reach.

There was a nasty pleasure in the ugly twist of Moran's lips as he supervised every detail of the binding of his foe.

'Moriarty,' I declared in a voice brittle with grief and fury, 'whatever your other crimes, for this act alone you will be damned for all eternity.'

The professor did not spare me as much as a glance as Moran's party clambered up to rejoin us. He beckoned forward another soldier, a tall man with a scar running from his brow to his chin that bespoke a life of unbridled violence. He was armed with a high-powered rifle, which he carried with the ease of a practised marksman.

Gazing down like a Roman emperor seated above an arena, Moriarty addressed my chained friend. 'Mr Holmes, Keller here will keep watch until the very end to ensure that nothing interferes with your execution. He is the best shot in the whole company, so you will perhaps beg him to end your life quickly. I leave the choice up to you. And now, farewell, Sherlock Holmes. We shall not meet again.'

As I was forced reluctantly away, I caught a final glimpse of Holmes bound to that ghastly rock, the cold waters rising to engulf him. I reflected with a heavy heart that if I should survive this dreadful adventure, it would be my sad duty to write the epitaph of a friend whom I shall ever regard as the best and wisest man I have ever known.

24

ONE LAST PROBLEM

How to describe the almost unendurable misery of my subsequent imprisonment? Dr MacReady and I were separated, denied the opportunity even to console each other. Shut away in our cell of the night before, all I could do was pace the floor and lament that Holmes had fallen so easily into the clutches of a man bent upon his destruction.

Was there any hope? I could see none. The chain was clearly unbreakable, the padlock so far out of reach that even if Holmes had the key it would do him no good. And then there was the marksman with the rifle, ready to end Holmes's life with a bullet if he should even find the means to attempt an escape.

Without either watch or clock, I had no way to measure the passing of time, but it felt like an eternity of utter anguish. I had no doubt of my own eventual fate once Moriarty decided that even as a hostage I was of no further use to him. For some indeterminate passage of hours I lay on the bed, staring up at the bare ceiling, my weary mind filled with memories: of Mary, of my first meeting with Holmes, of my dearest Gail – so far away that she might never learn what had become of me.

I was so lost in my melancholy reflections that I scarcely reacted when I heard a key turn in the lock and the door swung open. A uniformed figure entered and I assumed the worst.

'What have you come for?' I demanded. 'Am I now to be done away with also?'

The man's response gave me the biggest surprise of my life.

'Really, Watson, I expected a warmer welcome than that.'

My heart leapt at the sound of his voice. I leapt up from the bed and crossed the room in a bound. 'Holmes!'

For indeed there was that noble, hawk-like face gazing at me from beneath the peak of his soldier's cap. In unbounded delight I clapped him warmly on both shoulders.

He smiled. 'Not a ghost, I assure you, old fellow.'

'But how? This is impossible!'

'Outwitting Professor Moriarty presented considerable obstacles, to be sure, but *impossible* is too strong a word.' He nodded at the door. 'Perhaps you would be so good as to help me drag inside the guard I have rendered unconscious in the passage out there?'

Once we had hauled the senseless soldier inside and closed the door, I regarded my friend with an astonishment surpassing anything I had experienced before.

'Holmes, you cannot let this pass without explanation. You were trapped in conditions of certain death.'

'I shall be happy to render an account of my resurrection,' said Holmes, 'but while I do so, I would ask you to put on this man's uniform. It may prove a little snug, but it will serve.'

It was an easy matter to strip the outer garments from the unconscious guard, and while I changed clothing, my friend quickly told me his story.

'Our visit to Hunterswood granted me an opportunity to observe Professor Moriarty at close quarters for the first time, to assess at first hand both his strengths and his weaknesses. This allowed me to form a strategy by which he might be overcome.'

'He certainly seems to have developed remarkable powers of prediction,' I commented.

'That much is true,' Holmes agreed, 'but his forecasts tend to go awry when strong emotions are in play. Witness Price's unforeseen attack. I knew Moriarty would be expecting us to arrive here and would have planned our capture. So the task before me was to have a further move of my own already in place.'

'But Holmes, how did persuading him to chain you to that ghastly rock lead to your escape?'

Holmes allowed himself a small smile. 'You will recall, Watson, that during that matter of the Murdered Mediums, I made the acquaintance of the renowned American stage magician who is also the world's greatest escape artist. From him I learned two vital lessons: first, the importance of being able to hold one's breath for long periods of time. Second, when escaping from some trap, as our magician friend was wont to do from packing cases and even milk churns, it is absolutely essential to rig the imprisoning device beforehand in a way that is invisible to the casual eye but allows the possibility of escape.'

The military trousers were indeed uncomfortably snug, and as I secured the belt around my waist I queried, 'But the chain, Holmes? The padlock?'

'All perfectly explicable. Yesterday morning, when making my reconnaissance of the island from Munroe's fishing boat, I slipped into the water and swam to the Dead Man's Pool. Being able to swim under water for long stretches helped me to pass unobserved by any of the men patrolling the island. I had with me a chisel which I used to loosen one of the rings fixed to the rock.'

'And that was not noticed by the men who chained you?' I pulled on the soldier's tunic.

'I made sure my tamperings were subtle enough to defy detection,' Holmes explained. 'Once chained, I had only to wait until the tide had risen high enough for me to duck my head under and begin a series of tugs which pulled that single ring away from the rock, causing the chain to loosen and set me free. None of this was visible to the watcher Moriarty had set over me. I swam away and only surfaced at a spot where some rocks concealed me from view.'

I paused in the middle of buttoning the collar of my tunic and could not help reproaching him. 'But, Holmes, you gave me no inkling of any of this. For heaven's sake, you let me think you were dead! Have you any notion of what I've been through?'

'I am deeply sorry to have caused you such distress,' Holmes responded with utter sincerity, 'but it was vital that your reactions be authentic in order to deceive Moriarty into believing his triumph was complete.'

'But what a dreadful risk to take, Holmes. Your whole scheme hinged upon Moriarty's following your suggested method of execution and it could so easily have gone wrong.'

'As I said, Watson, I observed our adversary closely during our meeting with him at Hunterswood, and I had judged him well. I played on his vanity and sense of cruelty to excellent effect.'

My own injured feelings gave way to admiration for my friend's ingenuity and daring. 'As skilfully as you play upon the violin,' I added quietly.

Holmes gave an appreciative chuckle. 'A very apt metaphor.'

We tore the sheets from my bed and used them to bind and gag our prisoner. As we did so, Holmes continued his account of his miraculous reappearance.

'When the guard started back to the fortress to report on my demise, I was close on his trail. I took him from behind, catching him around the throat in a hold that swiftly rendered him unconscious. I then took his uniform for a disguise and used my own wet garments to tie him up and gag him. I left him in a hollow among thick bushes where he will not be found for some time.'

'Even dressed as one of Moran's brigade,' I pointed out, 'it is remarkable that you have come this far unchallenged.'

Holmes dismissed the matter with a shrug. 'A brute like Moran inspires neither loyalty nor discipline. His troops had been on a long night alert awaiting our arrival on the island, but with me apparently dead and you securely imprisoned, they immediately became slack and careless. From this point on, all you and I have to do is march along in a soldierly manner, as though on our way to carry out some fresh order, and no one will pay us any mind at all.'

We left the cell, locking it behind us, and pulled the peaks of our caps down as far as we could to obscure our features. Holmes took the lead along the passage and up the stairs.

'Holmes, where exactly are we going?' I inquired in a cautious undertone.

'To stop Moriarty's thinking machine,' he replied in a hushed voice, 'before it delivers to him the power he craves.'

'But an equation that will give him control of history itself? Is such a thing even possible or is it just the sick delusion of an unbalanced mind?'

'It sounds mad, I agree. But Moriarty's remarkable brain has reached such rarefied heights of mathematical abstraction, I fear we cannot take a chance. The machine must be stopped.'

As we walked along I remembered the triple lock and the vault door beyond that we would have to penetrate to reach the gigantic calculator. 'But, Holmes, how do you expect to—'

He signalled me to silence as two soldiers passed along a cross-passage ahead of us, talking in loud voices of how they proposed to spend the rewards they had been promised for their service. Their intentions were as ignoble as their language but they paid us no heed and disappeared round a corner.

The attitude of those men confirmed Holmes's assessment of the state of alertness of the garrison of Errinsay. Eventually, however, the absence of the guards captured and bound by Holmes and myself would be noticed and the alarm sounded.

We arrived at the first door without being challenged and Holmes immediately made examination of the three locks, pulling from his pocket a set of lock-picks as he did so.

'Stand lookout while I work,' he instructed. 'If anyone approaches, you must hail him with the bluff camaraderie of a fellow soldier, and as soon as he comes close subdue him as silently as possible.'

'Where did you obtain those special tools?' I inquired. 'We were thoroughly searched after our capture.'

Holmes flashed me a half smile as he began to manipulate the first lock. 'When I made my swim out to the Dead Man's Pool yesterday,' he replied, beginning his work on the first lock, 'I took with me a waterproof pouch containing a few items that were certain to prove useful. I concealed it in a crevice in the rocks and retrieved it after freeing myself from the chain.'

He returned his full attention to the task at hand while I kept anxious watch on the far end of the passage, my ears alert for the sound of approaching feet. As the seconds ticked away, I counted it fortunate that with his only dangerous enemy disposed of, Moriarty had not seen fit to place a guard over the well-secured entrance to his machine chamber. Within the space of a few minutes, a grunt of satisfaction told me that Holmes had disposed of all three locks. It was with some relief that I joined him in the inner passage where we were concealed by the door.

Before us now stood the heavy steel barrier with its combination lock. It looked, if anything, more impenetrable than I remembered.

'Surely it will be impossible to go any further without the combination,' I pointed out. 'And our view was blocked the whole time Moriarty was working the dial.'

Holmes silenced me with an upraised finger, then shut his eyes in rapt concentration. His lips moved in unspoken thought and I could only wonder by what extraordinary mental effort he expected to conjure the combination out of the air.

He placed a hand on the dial and with the utmost concentration began to turn it back and forth, noting the satisfying click of the tumblers falling into place as he did so. As he worked, he explained, 'Though I could not see the movements of the dial, each turn is accompanied by an almost imperceptible series of clicks. To ears as sharp as mine, however, they were just barely audible and I committed to memory the number of clicks in each turn.'

'But since the initial position of the dial was hidden from our view,' I objected, 'you are still operating blindly.'

'Not so,' Holmes demurred. 'Although Moriarty was careful to allow no glimpse of the dial when working the combination, when we exited and he closed the door, I was able to glimpse the final setting. From that I was able to calculate backwards to the start position.'

My astonishment at this feat of perception and memory was only increased when Holmes made the final twist. Leaning on the handle, he hauled the great metal door open. There before us lay the impenetrable glass screen with the colossal machine beyond, working through its relentless cogitation. The clicks and screeches of its operation sounded to me now like the wicked chattering of a horde of infernal imps.

'What now, Holmes?' I wondered. 'Even if we had the tools to do it, there is no way to get at the thing to shut it down.'

Holmes walked up to the elaborate keyboard and flexed his long fingers like a concert pianist preparing himself for a performance. 'It is not for mere amusement that I spent the last few days studying Professor Kilbane's notebook,' he said. 'I have in that time mastered the mathematical language necessary to communicate with one of his machines. Before this electronic colossus completes the task programmed by Moriarty, I have one final problem to set before it.'

25

A DESPERATE DUEL

I stared through the glass at the gargantuan construct of steel, circuits and lights that lay beyond the protective barrier. The clatter of its operation beat upon my ear like the inexorable thunder of a rolling juggernaut.

'Can you not simply command it to cease its calculations?' I suggested.

Holmes studied the elaborate keyboard, his fingers floating lightly above it. 'Moriarty has made it quite clear that his demand for that all-encompassing algorithm cannot be countermanded or directly interfered with. If I am correct, however, there is nothing to prevent me from setting an additional problem before this mechanical brain, such is its vast computational power.'

Holmes's intent was still not clear to me. 'And what exactly will that achieve?'

I received no reply. Instead my friend began tapping on the keys with the speed and precision of an experienced typist. The rhythmic clicking of the keyboard sounded to me like a very small thing compared to the daunting din of the machine's spinning cylinders, rattling switches and whirling rolls of tape, and I could not help but liken it to David's puny slingshot pitted against the armoured giant Goliath.

I observed in awestruck silence this struggle of the greatest intellect I have known pitted against the evil genius of Moriarty and the dreadful mechanical brain he had created to serve his relentless ambition.

I could tell from the tensed hunch of his shoulders, the rapid, almost convulsive, movements of his fingers, and the beads of sweat breaking out upon his large brow that Holmes was engaged in a ferocious feat of absolute concentration. He paused only occasionally to call to mind a particular page or line from Kilbane's notebook which he had expended such effort in memorising.

At last, with a deliberate punch of the final key, Holmes completed his coded instructions and stepped back, rubbing his temple with a thin, pale finger. He took a deep breath and turned to face me.

'There, it is done,' he declared.

'Holmes, I still don't follow you. What exactly have you done?'

'You will recall from your history, Watson, that protesting French workers in the nineteenth century were reputed to have thrown their wooden shoes – their *sabots* – into the industrial machinery of their employers in order to disrupt production. Well, I have hurled my shoe into Moriarty's machinery and I can only hope it is enough to sabotage his plans.'

I could perceive no alteration in the furious activity of the gigantic calculator and still had no clue as to what Holmes expected to result from his efforts. As mystified as ever, I asked, 'Might I inquire as to the exact nature of this shoe?'

'Have you ever heard of Scarletti's Theorem? No?' Prompted by my bafflement, he poured out a quick and concise explanation. 'Scarletti's Theorem is a notorious mathematical conundrum that has driven some of the finest minds in the field close to despair. In fact it can only be solved by making the assumption that one and zero have the same value, a conclusion which undermines the basis of rationality itself. The human mind has a flexibility which allows it, however unwillingly, to encompass even so demanding a paradox as this, but a machine intelligence lacks that all-important human element.'

I was struggling to absorb these very abstract concepts when Holmes clapped me briskly on the shoulder. 'Come, Watson. We must get away from here before anyone suspects what we are up to. And we must rescue Dr MacReady before the alarm is raised.'

I was only too glad to put as much distance as possible between ourselves and the furious bedlam of Moriarty's mathematical engine. As we threaded our way back through the fortress we were careful to walk with confident strides while keeping to the shadows as much as possible in order to obscure our features. One clear glimpse of our faces might be enough to give us away.

Fortunately for us, Moran had selected for his special brigade men with a liking for violence, and upon such brutes military discipline never has more than a feeble grip. With their commander celebrating his capture of the intruders by the usual indulgent excesses, and Moriarty focused entirely upon the imminent delivery of his final predictive formula, these men reverted to a careless laxity typical of the backstreet thug. Those we spotted appeared to be wandering unsteadily from one source of food and alcohol to another. We heard coarse songs echoing down distant corridors and here and there outbreaks of intoxicated discord.

When we emerged into the courtyard we found it empty except for a group of men playing cards in a far corner below the west tower. A lone guard at the gate was slouched upon a stool with a cigarette dangling sleepily from his lip.

'Only a short way to go now,' Holmes murmured as we strolled towards the exit, doing our best to show no signs of haste. I was just wondering how long our luck would hold when a uniformed figure stepped out of a doorway and grabbed me by the arm. I raised a reflexive fist, then froze at the sound of a familiar voice.

'Really, doctor, is that any way to greet a lady?'

To my utter amazement I was face to face with Dr MacReady, easily recognisable even though, like us, she was dressed in the uniform and cap of one of the island's garrison.

'Dr MacReady!' I gasped. I was so taken aback I could not think what else to say.

'Why so surprised?' she asked. 'Do you not mind that I've dressed up as a soldier before?'

Holmes drew close and barely kept himself from reaching out to touch her. 'Well, this is most gratifying,' was his restrained comment.

Dr MacReady measured him with a look of mingled surprise and amusement. 'Mr Holmes, I'm glad to find you hale and hearty and not even a wee bit damp.'

'A full account of my resurrection will have to wait for the present,' said Holmes. 'But how do you come to be free?'

'Well, they had me shut away in a lab in one of those huts out there with one of Moran's brutes standing guard over me. He'd no way of telling, though, that instead of working on a weapon for his boss, I was concocting a means of escape, beginning with some knockout drops that I slipped into his coffee. He'll be sleeping that off for some considerable time, the great gowk.'

Holmes eyed her with undisguised admiration. 'And while he was unconscious . . .'

'I borrowed the uniform, just as the two of you have done.' There was a mischievous glint in her eye which reminded me of the schoolgirl pranks she and her old friend Ophelia Faith had been chortling over only a few days before. 'You'll have noticed things have got a bit lax around here, so I'd no trouble ducking my way into the castle in hopes of freeing Dr Watson.'

'Just as we were on our way to rescue you,' I said.

'We can congratulate each other on our resourcefulness later,' advised Holmes, leading the way across the courtyard. 'We need to get out of here while we still can, before—'

Even as he spoke a harsh blare of sirens broke out all around us. The din set the whole fortress on alert and all at once it became a hive of alarmed activity. The guard on the gate ahead of us jumped up from his stool, rifle in hand.

'Steady, steady,' Holmes encouraged us. 'We may still manage to bluff our way past.'

The guard did appear confused and I could see that if we simply kept walking, he might not connect us with the alarm going on all around. That hope was quickly dashed, however.

'Stop right where you are!' Moran's voice barked from behind us.

We halted and turned to face him. He was advancing

towards us at the head of a dozen of his soldiers, all with guns pointed directly at us. A feral amusement twisted his thick lips.

'Well, well, well. When I discovered Watson had escaped, I didn't guess it was with the help of a woman – and a ghost.' Moran let out a croak of dry laughter and confronted Holmes eye to eye. 'So, Holmes, however you saved your neck, at least it gives me the chance to finish you off the old-fashioned way. Bates, go and fetch my duelling sabres.'

The soldier obediently dashed off into one of the towers.

'Duelling sabres?' Dr MacReady echoed scornfully. 'Are we playing pirates now?'

Moran pointed his pistol at her. 'You keep your mouth shut, woman, or I'll see you roughly handled.'

'Really, Moran,' said Holmes, 'we already had our swordplay and the matter was decided.'

'You did well enough when we were just sporting,' Moran spat vengefully, 'but now we'll see how you fare with naked steel.'

'Moran, what the devil is going on?'

The angry question came from Professor Moriarty, who had emerged from the keep in a state of extreme wrath.

'We have two prisoners and a dead man running around loose,' Moran informed him in a loud, hard voice. 'If you'd left it to me they'd all be dead and buried by now.'

At the sight of Holmes, Moriarty staggered to a halt as if he beheld an apparition from beyond the grave. Even in the midst of our peril, I could tell that Holmes was relishing the moment.

'Does my reappearance leave you baffled, professor?' he asked. 'You certainly seem discomfited.'

Moriarty's jaw flexed tight and a nerve pulsed in his temple. 'There is only one possible explanation,' he grated. 'You visited that pool beforehand and somehow weakened one of the rings. Once the tide had risen high enough to conceal your actions from view, you were able to tug it loose and free yourself.'

'An admirable analysis,' said Holmes. 'How unfortunate for you that your powers of foresight failed to predict my plan in advance.'

'Unfortunate? For me?' Moriarty emitted a harsh laugh. 'This changes nothing. Once loose, you sought to free your friend Watson and Dr MacReady, an aim as futile as it was predictable. And it has all come to naught.'

'Do you really believe the rescue of your prisoners was my sole intent?' Holmes challenged.

'What else could you possibly . . . ?' Moriarty was silenced by an ominous reverberation of which we were all suddenly aware.

It began as a deep rumble, as of distant thunder, then rose rapidly in pitch and volume until it might have been taken for the agonised scream of some gigantic, subterranean beast. We could feel the vibrations beneath our feet and I knew they must be coming from the impenetrable underground chamber that housed Moriarty's devilish engine of electronic thought.

The professor was both bewildered and appalled. 'But how? *How?*' He stabbed a finger at Holmes. 'What have you done?'

Sherlock Holmes indulged in a dramatic pause then spoke one word as though it were the key to a magic spell. '*Scarletti*.'

Moriarty's eyes flew wide as though at the name of some monstrous beast that had been summoned to devour him. His flung back his head, his shoulders shook and his fingers clawed at the air. With a howl of anguish he spun about and dashed towards the keep, racing to halt the impending destruction of his creation.

How Holmes had achieved this was beyond my guessing, but Moriarty's horror was all the confirmation needed to show that his evil plans were crashing down in ruins thanks to the actions of his hated adversary.

Even as the professor disappeared into the castle's interior, the soldier Bates returned carrying two sheathed swords in his arms. Moran snatched them both and tossed one at Holmes's feet, where it hit the cobbled ground with a clatter. He yanked his own weapon clear of its scabbard and took a slash at the air.

'Now, Holmes,' he snarled, 'I'm done with playing the gentleman. Now we fight to the death!'

26

THE DEN OF THIEVES

'A duel to the death?' scoffed Dr MacReady. 'I've never heard anything so daft!'

'I couldn't agree more,' I concurred with feeling.

In spite of our misgivings, Holmes bent down to pick up the sword and accept the challenge. Moran made some practice passes with his sabre and bared his teeth in savage anticipation of blood-letting.

As Holmes's fingers touched the hilt of the sword at his feet, Dr MacReady commanded us in a low but emphatic voice, 'Gentlemen, please avert your gaze!'

Her tone carried such authority that Holmes and I instinctively obeyed. As I turned my head, from the corner of my eye I glimpsed her pulling from her pocket an object which she hurled to the ground in front of Moran and his men. It exploded in a flash of blinding white light that sent them reeling back, cursing in the most foul language.

Dr MacReady grabbed our elbows and launched us towards the gate. 'Magnesium flare,' she explained shortly. 'If you let a canny lass loose in a lab full of chemicals, you have to expect some mischief.'

Dazzled by the flash, the sole guard on duty made an ineffectual attempt to bar our path. Holmes levelled him with a solid punch to the jaw and we sped on our way with Moran's blasphemous oaths scorching the air behind us. Before us lay a scattered assembly of wooden huts adjoining the castle walls. As we passed them by, one of them exploded in a ball of baleful fire.

'I thought it best to destroy every vestige of Price's work,' Dr MacReady explained. 'Don't worry about the sleeping guard. I dragged him well clear before setting the fuse.'

I could not help but be impressed by how thoroughly she had prepared and executed her own escape. Before I could express my sincerest approbation, Holmes anticipated me.

'I must compliment you on your ingenuity,' he told her warmly. 'I do, however, regret missing the opportunity to settle matters with Moran.'

'Really, Holmes, you are impossible!' I declared with some heat.

My friend made no rejoinder. Surveying the surrounding terrain, he assessed our bearings with a keen eye. To me it was a trackless wasteland of looming trees and prickly undergrowth, but Holmes swiftly made up his mind.

'This way!' he told us, striking out confidently through the scrub to our right.

Following after him, we entered a maze of brush and stunted evergreens. Up ahead, we caught occasional glimpses of the sea gilded by the westering sun.

'Given the impossibility of swimming to the mainland,' Dr MacReady remarked, 'I'm hoping you've got some plan in mind, Mr Holmes.'

Without breaking stride, he answered over his shoulder, 'In a short time, Dr MacReady, it is my intention that we should vanish into thin air, just as you did at Castle Dunfillan last year.'

'That should be a trick worth seeing,' said the doctor with a wry smile.

Presently we came to the vestiges of a path, which Holmes followed with evident satisfaction. Its winding course took us through fields of bracken and out on to a rocky headland. To my consternation, we appeared to have reached a dead end. Nothing daunted, Holmes beckoned us towards a gap between two jutting boulders at the very edge of what looked to be a sheer drop.

Joining him, I saw that the path continued steeply down a slanting rift in the cliff face. Descending, we arrived at a narrow ledge. Holmes fearlessly stepped out on to it and moved forward, leaving Dr MacReady and myself with no choice but to follow.

Directly below us, the incoming tide was dashing up sheets of spray among a cluster of jagged rocks. With a shudder, I wrenched my gaze away from the drop and pressed myself flat to the cliff. Here and there sparse clumps of outgrowth offered handholds, but I was only too aware that one minor misstep might spell disaster.

Halfway along the ledge was a rough layer of gorse. Holmes paused just beyond this spot and hauled the tangled screen aside to expose the cramped entrance to a cave. 'After you,' he invited.

All but dumbfounded, we squeezed through the gap and found ourselves in a rocky chamber the size of a modest living room. Entering behind us, Holmes fetched an oil lamp and some matches from an aperture. Once the lamp was lit I saw that the cave was crudely furnished with plank benches and a wooden packing case upon which Holmes placed the lantern.

'You explained to me how you concealed a few helpful items close to the Dead Man's Pool,' I said, 'but surely you had neither the time nor the means to set up this hideaway.'

'Of course not,' said Holmes. 'This den was established long ago as a hiding place for smugglers where they could conceal themselves and their contraband. It has been used intermittently since then by some of the locals.'

'Well, it's a snug wee hidey-hole, to be sure,' said Dr MacReady. Taking a seat on one of the benches, she shook her russet hair free of the military cap which she happily tossed aside.

'It was Geordie Munroe who told you about this place,' I guessed.

'How to find it and what were the few comforts it contained,' Holmes affirmed as he drew the concealing screen back over the cave entrance. 'I considered it to be impolite to ask him what use he had made of it himself.'

Looking around, I spotted some bottles of beer, tinned meats and dry biscuit stored here by the last occupants for their own comfort. I was glad to see that we would neither starve nor go thirsty during our sojourn.

'Whoever that friend of yours is,' said Dr MacReady, 'I'll forgive him any illegal capers in exchange for the use of his hidden nook.'

Holmes turned the lamp down to its lowest setting so that we became no more than vague, dark outlines to each other. 'It is possible that someone among Moran's men may have sufficient tracking skills to follow our trail to this end of the island,' he explained in an undertone, 'so we must be careful not to give ourselves away by any detectable light or noise.'

I indulged in a rueful but invisible smile. 'In all our long association, I never expected that we would one day become fugitives from the law then end up taking refuge in a den of thieves such as this.'

'If the two of you have been running from the law,' said Dr MacReady, 'then you must have quite a tale to tell me.'

Before the story could be told, Holmes hushed us. Listening intently, I soon made out what it was that his keen ears had already perceived – the rough voices of men calling out to each other somewhere beyond the cliff edge above our heads.

'Fortunately, from up there is no sign of any possible place of concealment,' Holmes whispered, 'and the perilous nature of the path should discourage any exploration of the cliff face.'

I fervently hoped he was right, for I had no doubt as to our fate should we be discovered. After the reverses they had suffered this day, neither Moriarty nor Moran would indulge in duels or slow methods of execution. We would almost certainly be shot on sight.

We maintained an anxious silence for as long as we could hear the distant sounds of the searchers, and even when these passed away we remained cautious in our speech and movements.

'Perhaps, Mr Holmes,' Dr MacReady suggested, 'if you can do so *sotto voce*, it would help to pass the time if you would tell me how you and Dr Watson found your way to this bleak place.'

Holmes obliged by telling the doctor of what had occurred since her abduction, assuring her that her friend Ophelia Faith was safe and well. I occasionally interrupted his dry, factual account of our adventures to add some detail that he had omitted on the basis that it was only of the most frivolous interest.

Holmes concluded with a further explanation of how he had sabotaged Moriarty's great machine. 'It was you, Watson, who gave me the idea when you suggested that the explosion at Hunterswood might have been caused by the Velox machine's overheating.'

'I'm glad to have provided some measure of inspiration,' I said, 'but I don't quite grasp how it applies to a mathematical puzzle.'

'As I explained before,' said Holmes, 'any attempt to solve Scarletti's Theorem leads to the conclusion that one and zero have the same value. The human brain running up against such a paradox has a certain resilience in coping with it. A machine intelligence, however, operates digitally, meaning it is entirely dependent for its function on the absolute certainty that one and zero are two distinctly different values. Consequently any attempt by the machine to solve Scarletti's Theorem, as I had instructed it to do, was doomed to fail, forcing it to divert more and more of its computational power into answering an impossible question.'

'Hence the ghastly sounds of mechanical distress which threw Moriarty into such a panic,' I recalled.

'By that time, I doubt there was anything he could do to halt the wreckage of his calculator,' said Holmes.

'It sounds to me, Mr Holmes, that what you're describing

there is a complete mental breakdown,' commented Dr MacReady.

'While it is misleading to ascribe emotional states to a machine,' said Holmes, 'I suppose it is not an inaccurate analogy.'

'Is the damage beyond repair, do you think?' I asked.

Holmes pondered a moment. 'I'm sure Moriarty has skilled electrical engineers among his staff here, probably under duress. How long it would take them to set the machine running again is impossible to estimate without examining it.'

'And are we just to sit here while he sets his plan in motion again?' demanded Dr MacReady. She sounded as if she was prepared to launch an immediate assault on Donald o' the Dirk's castle, with or without our support.

'For the present that's all we can do,' Holmes answered calmly. 'Soon it will be night and no searchers will risk approaching the cliff edge in the dark. So I think we have nothing to worry about until morning when we must maintain the utmost caution. Moriarty will realise that we have a hiding place and the search will be intensified.'

'Could we not sneak out and steal a boat from somewhere on this rock?' Dr MacReady suggested.

'That might be worth a try,' I agreed.

I saw Holmes's head shake in the gloom. 'We are all much too tired to attempt anything so hazardous. Our best course for now is to get a good night's rest.'

Some straw matting and rough blankets were all the bedding available, but it was still a blessing not to spend the night in captivity, however restricted our new freedom might be. I slept surprisingly well under the circumstances, but awoke with stiffness in my back and limbs.

We breakfasted on the unappetising supplies left by the smugglers and contemplated a long day huddled here in the gloom. Such was not to be our fate, however, because we soon heard voices from somewhere above. I strained to make out the words, hoping that they would simply pass by.

'Blimey! You couldn't get a goat to crawl along there!' one man exclaimed.

'You know old egg-head's orders,' another told him. 'Every scrap of ground's got to be searched. Look, we'll tie a rope round you before we send you down.'

'You'd better keep a good grip,' the first man declared. 'I don't want to end up as fish food.'

I exchanged an anxious glance with my companions. It seemed certain that our refuge was about to be exposed.

27

A TIGHT CORNER

I was only too aware that while our hiding place would escape detection from above, anyone daring the narrow path and making a thorough probe of the bracken-clad cliff face would inevitably discover us.

'What are the odds of our making it down to the shore?' Dr MacReady asked in a whisper.

'Impossible,' Holmes replied. 'The path gives out only a little further on and the drop to the rocks below is a lethal one.'

From outside we could hear the sounds of further discussion and the scraping of boots on stone.

'If one man comes upon us, we could surely overpower him,' I suggested. 'And it would be difficult to launch any sort of assault against us on so tight a front.'

'That might buy us a little time,' Holmes conceded, 'but only until Moriarty contrived a way to flush us out with fire or gas.'

'He has an ample supply of both,' said Dr MacReady ruefully.

'We must retreat as far as we can and extinguish the lantern,' Holmes decided. 'That is our best hope of escaping detection, that and a certain inefficiency on the part of our pursuers.'

We obeyed this instruction, crouching low in the deepest recess of the little cave. Plunged into darkness, we could only listen to the searcher moving carefully down the treacherous path.

'Spotted anything?' called a voice from above.

'I'll be lucky if I don't break my ruddy neck!' the unhappy scout yelled back.

The sound of his shuffling feet drew closer and I tensed for action. It occurred to me that I might shove him over the edge in such a way that his companions above might think he had fallen by accident and lose their grip on the rope. It felt like a cowardly way to kill a man, however, and I hoped I would not be driven to it.

Now came the noise of a knife or bayonet scraping about among the bracken and our exposure appeared inevitable. The three of us were holding our breath and pressing hard against the rocky rear of our hidey-hole. It was then that there came a bellow from above.

'Here, did you hear that?'

Other cries of alarm were also raised.

'What's going on?' the searcher demanded. He had halted only inches from the cave entrance. 'What's all the ruckus?'

'Don't you hear the guns from down there?' a voice responded.

'Hey, that was a bleedin' cannon!' exclaimed another.

'Right, I'm coming up!' announced the searcher. 'Does anybody know what the hell's going on?'

We kept stock still, unwilling to risk our luck until we were sure all danger of discovery had passed. Presently we heard from overhead voices and footfalls fading into the distance. With a sigh of relief Holmes relit the lantern, the glow revealing a hawkish grin on his lean features.

'That was about as close a shave as I can recall,' he said.

'Another few seconds . . .' I gasped. I was grateful to have been spared the decision of whether or not to send a man tumbling helplessly down to his doom on the rocks below.

'I've no doubt Ophelia would ascribe it to the workings of a benevolent providence,' said Dr MacReady, 'and at this point I wouldn't be minded to argue.'

'I think we can attribute this turn of events to an entity somewhat less exalted than the Almighty,' Holmes remarked with a thin smile.

'Mycroft!' It came to me in a flash. 'That letter you left with Lestrade to be handed to your brother upon his return.'

'Yes, Watson,' Holmes affirmed. 'It told him where I had stored the documentary evidence exposing Moriarty's many crimes. It also contained the exact location of Avalon and the name of Geordie Munroe as man to be contacted.'

'So all along you've been expecting a rescue!' Dr MacReady scolded, but with a twinkle in her eye. 'You might have told us.'

'I didn't wish to raise false hopes,' said Holmes. 'It was by no means certain that help would arrive in time to save us from Moriarty's vengeance. Though I made clear to Mycroft the importance of haste, the professor has agents in Whitehall who might yet have thrown obstacles in the way of his efforts.'

'I suppose it's safe for us to go outside now?' I suggested.

Holmes nodded. 'But be careful. There will be a battle

raging up there and there is always the chance of a stray bullet's flying in our direction.'

He led the way, drawing aside the concealing screen and setting a cautious foot on the path outside. We ascended slowly, breathing in the fresh sea air and enjoying the warmth of the sun on our faces. Once up on the clifftop we gazed towards the north where the noise of gunfire was coming from the castle. Off to the east I could see a Royal Navy frigate standing by and I assumed there were other vessels hidden by the rising ground.

'Are we going back to the castle?' I asked.

'No, we have more important business,' said Holmes. 'We know Moriarty has a seaplane and, according to Geordie, there is only one place where it can be concealed – a cove on the western shore surrounded by hills.'

'So if that devil Moriarty is making his escape,' said Dr MacReady, 'you think that's where we'll find him?'

'I'm certain of it,' said Holmes, setting off at a brisk trot. 'He only has a small force here and cannot hold out for long against a full military assault. Flight will be his only option.'

'I only hope we're in time,' I said, matching my friend's pace, with Dr MacReady keeping well up at our side. It would be a bitter pill to swallow if, after all we had endured, that evil genius should manage to evade justice.

Bounding over the dry heather and brushing our way through thorny tangles of wild greenery, we scrambled at last up a rocky hillside. From the summit we looked down on the hidden cove where we saw a seaplane bobbing a few hundred yards from shore. A motorised dinghy was speeding towards the plane, steered by one of the island's security brigade. Even at this distance there was no mistaking the passenger – Professor Moriarty.

'If only we had a rifle,' I said, 'we might be able to stop him.'

Almost as if he had overheard me, Moriarty looked up and fixed his reptilian gaze upon us. He raised a closed hand above his head and waved it in the air.

'Look, Holmes,' I observed. 'He's shaking his fist at us. Rather a petty gesture, don't you think?'

'You misinterpret him, Watson,' Holmes corrected me. 'He is brandishing the remaining vial of phlogiston to demonstrate that he still possesses it and that it will be his instrument of revenge.'

'Really? Are you sure?'

'Quite sure.' Holmes's features tightened. 'Matters are not yet settled between us.'

'Well, I say good riddance to that black-hearted loon,' said Dr MacReady. 'I hope all he finds for himself is a watery grave.'

By now Moriarty was clambering aboard the plane with the soldier behind him. The door slammed and the propellers roared into life. We could only watch helplessly as the plane skimmed across the waves and rose up into the western sky. As it dwindled into the distance I saw the grave concern in my friend's face.

'Not to worry, Holmes,' I assured him. 'Moriarty has lost his base of operations and now that he is exposed as a criminal all the resources he commanded will have been removed.'

'As long as he is free,' my friend responded, 'he will yet contrive a final throw of the dice.'

'Come, Mr Holmes,' Dr MacReady encouraged him, 'let's at least celebrate your victory over that evil man and the fact that we're all still alive to see it.'

'As you say,' Holmes agreed, 'we have some reason to be cheerful.' He paused to cock an ear and said, 'Since the sounds of battle have ceased, I think we can take it that the castle is now in friendly hands.'

We trekked back to that grim fortress in a very different spirit from that which had accompanied our escape. As we climbed the rocky ground I was able to make out a total of three Royal Navy vessels anchored offshore. Parties of soldiers in the distinctive colours of the Royal Marines were making a thorough search of the various outbuildings, freeing the imprisoned scientists and engineers and flushing out any remaining members of Moran's brigade. The castle itself had been secured and from the open gateway a distinctive figure was coming to meet us.

I could not have been more astonished if King George himself had made an appearance, for advancing majestically towards us was a man who could hardly bear to leave the comfort of his armchair – Mycroft Holmes.

28

THE HUNT RESUMES

Noting the surprise on our faces, Mycroft Holmes drew himself up haughtily and raised a hand to keep us from speaking.

'Yes, I know. Having dedicated many years to establishing a routine of physical inertia as the counterpoint to my extreme intellectual activity, it pains me to be discovered acting out of character. However, given the importance of this operation and the lives at stake, I could hardly afford to risk its being bungled. I am, therefore, here by necessity to issue orders in person.'

'However extraordinary the circumstances, Mycroft,' said Holmes, 'I have never been so glad to see you.'

Mycroft peered peevishly down his nose. 'Let us be frank, Sherlock. You have never been glad to see me, at least not since the celebrated occasion when I absolutely forbade you to interfere in the matter of Madame Zarevsky's memoir.'

'For reasons that did neither you nor the British Crown any credit,' Holmes returned sharply.

Mycroft's already imposing frame appeared to swell up with sheer indignation. 'My position is such that I cannot afford to indulge those trifles of conscience which you are wont to entertain, dear brother. We can only be grateful that, in spite of your stubborn prying, a scandal was avoided at the last.'

'Gentlemen, surely this is not an appropriate time to be rehashing old grievances,' I intervened.

'You are, as ever, the peacemaker, Dr Watson,' Mycroft conceded with a small bow. 'And you are quite correct. Your past indiscretions, Sherlock, are as nothing compared to this latest escapade.'

'I assure you it was not my intention to subject you to any manner of inconvenience,' Holmes asserted drily.

Mycroft glowered at him. 'I leave the country for only a few weeks – and that under duress, I might add – and when I return, what do I find? People have been bursting into flames, Hunterswood has been dispersed, and you and Dr Watson have become fugitives from the law. I hope the prime minister will bear this in mind the next time he seeks to drag me from the comfort of my own office.'

'However out of character it may be, Mr Holmes,' said Dr MacReady, 'you've certainly come charging to the rescue in the nick of time.'

'Ah, this must be Dr MacReady.' Mycroft made as much of a bow as his physique permitted. 'I'm glad to see that you appear none the worse for your ordeal.'

The doctor tucked a stray lock of russet hair back into place and gave a wry smile. 'My mother was always telling me a that spot of vigorous exercise never did a body any harm.'

'A philosophy I do not share,' said Mycroft, suppressing a shudder. He turned back to his brother. 'We have so far unearthed no trace of Professor Moriarty. Can you enlighten me as to his whereabouts?'

When Holmes recounted how the professor had made his escape Mycroft uttered a grunt of displeasure. 'That is troubling. The man knows far too much to be running around loose.'

'I couldn't agree more,' said Holmes. 'You can count on me to spare no effort in tracking him down.'

'I would expect no less.'

'You must have been aware of Moriarty's role as director of Hunterswood,' I said. 'Did you have no suspicion of him?'

'I am embarrassed to admit I did not,' Mycroft confessed. 'In my own defence I must point out that I do not personally vet every appointment and I have been much distracted. Accommodating the demands of our American allies has proved no trifling matter.'

'Do you think, Mr Holmes,' Dr MacReady asked Mycroft, 'we might go inside now? I'd like to have a wash and maybe rustle up some hot food.'

'Of course. Forgive my bad manners,' said Mycroft. 'I am unused to entertaining, particularly under conditions such as these.'

As we entered the courtyard we were passed by a column of prisoners being escorted down to the shore where they were to board the launches that would transfer them to the waiting ships. We were informed by the captain in charge that Colonel Sebastian Moran was not among the captured soldiers, leaving us to speculate as to whether he was aboard the seaplane with his master or had arranged a separate escape of his own.

Several intelligence officers were examining the boxes of files and folders being brought outside to determine which should be taken away and which destroyed. The victory of His Majesty's forces over the ill-disciplined louts of Moran's brigade appeared to have been swift and complete.

While Mycroft accompanied Dr MacReady to the castle's living quarters, Holmes and I descended to the chamber where Moriarty's great machine was stored. The protective glass screen had been blown apart by explosives, laying bare the ruined mechanism beyond.

The havoc wrought by Holmes's ruse had been augmented by further acts of destruction engineered by Moriarty to place the machine beyond any possibility of restoration. The professor had clearly resolved that no legacy should be left behind of his and Kilbane's achievements in the field of mechanical intelligence.

'It's a sad loss,' Holmes commented. 'Human progress might have been advanced immeasurably by this new technology.'

I felt compelled to disagree. 'Personally, Holmes, I think we are well rid of anything that can be turned to such evil ends as Moriarty had in mind.'

With that we turned our backs on the wreckage of the professor's mad dream of the enslavement of mankind.

I have rarely been so delighted to return to the homely comforts of Baker Street as I was at the end of the long train journey back from Scotland. Our experiences on Errinsay had taken a physical and emotional toll that made it doubly pleasurable to sink into our familiar armchairs and await the arrival of an afternoon tea prepared by the skilled hands of Mrs Hudson. Dr MacReady had agreed to join us before returning to the scientific work that had been interrupted by her involvement in the affair of the Devil's Blaze.

Setting those harrowing experiences thoroughly behind us, it was a welcome relaxation to speak of less weighty matters. We talked of our travels, our musical interests and the various merits of our favourite authors. It was an hour happily spent and I had never before seen Holmes find such enjoyment in the company of a woman. I knew that beneath the austere façade he affected, his emotions ran as deep as those of any man, and it had long been my hope that one day he would give them freer rein for the sake of his own happiness.

At last the time of departure arrived and we all stood.

'Mr Holmes, working with you has been very interesting,' said Dr MacReady. 'I might almost say exhilarating.'

She offered her hand and Holmes shook it in a gesture of professional respect. 'Renewing our brief acquaintance has indeed proved a distinct pleasure.'

As she moved to leave, Dr MacReady paused in the doorway to look back. 'If you feel the need to contact me in future, for any reason at all, I'm sure you'll know how to find me.'

'Indeed I shall.'

The door closed and we heard her footsteps descending the stairway to the street outside. Holmes flung himself into his armchair and reached for a newspaper. I snatched it away and tossed it aside, much to his consternation.

'Holmes, is that all you have to say to the lady?'

He appeared genuinely puzzled. 'What more would you have me say?'

I eyed him sternly. 'Holmes, I never thought I should have the occasion to say this to you, but you are a fool.'

I noted a perceptible flinch. 'I find that rather uncalled for,' he responded stiffly.

'Good heavens, man! She saved both our lives!'

'I believe I have expressed my appreciation of that fact.'

Taking a deep breath, I decided to renew my assault upon his complacency from a different angle. 'Tell me, do you expect ever again to encounter a lady of such intelligence, courage and resourcefulness?'

'I should say the odds are very much against such an eventuality.'

'Then how, by all that's holy, can you simply let her walk out of your life, perhaps forever?'

There was an extended pause during which Holmes appeared to be digesting the import of my words. A tiny crease formed between his brows, which in my mind I likened to the first crack in a fortress wall under artillery bombardment. At length he spoke.

'Do I understand that you wish me to enter into some sort of romantic liaison with the lady?'

By this point I could scarcely contain my exasperation. 'You might at least invite her to dinner. Is that too much to expect? I believe you would find her to be a kindred spirit. You may not be aware of it, but she, like you, lost someone especially dear to her in the last war. She too has long believed that particular door to be closed.'

Holmes fixed me with a scrutinising stare. 'It is

possible that you mean well, Watson, but I can't avoid the suspicion that you are seeking some means to ease your own conscience, so that when you abandon me for your new life with Miss Preston you will not feel any pang of regret at leaving me here in desolate loneliness.'

I could not deny that he might have scored a point there, but I was not to be diverted. 'Certainly I do not wish to see this apartment become a museum and you one of the exhibits. Such an end would not be worthy of you.'

Holmes sighed deeply and spread his hands before him. 'My life, outside of your welcome support and companionship, has been one of solitude and danger. Surely that is no environment for a woman, no matter how capable she may be.'

'It need not always be so,' I persisted. 'With your many gifts you could in the future find other avenues of employment – music, or pure scientific research, for example.'

'You are talking about retirement.' He shook his head. 'I foresee no such leisure for me, no peaceful twilight. A career like mine can end in only one way and I believe that will involve a final confrontation with Professor Moriarty.'

'Moriarty? Then you do mean to hunt him down?'

'That is my fixed intent.'

'But how? Where?'

'You surely did not think he had retired to a villa somewhere to lick his wounds?' Holmes clapped a hand down on the arm of his chair. 'No, the professor is active as never before, playing his final card to the best advantage.'

'I assume you refer to that one remaining vial of phlogiston. But surely he no longer has the resources at his command to develop it into the weapon he described to us.'

'A form of the fiery compound that could be dispersed over a wide area, exposing whole populations to its dire effects, with ignition at his radio command. That was indeed his ambition.'

'To achieve that would take a team of expert scientists and a huge well-equipped laboratory, all of which have been taken away from him.'

'Which is why his plan will be to sell the phlogiston to someone who has all those facilities and more at his command and would pay almost any price to lay his hands on so potentially devastating a weapon.'

'You are referring, I take it, to Hitler. Yes, that madman would take a sick delight in wielding that sort of power.'

'With sufficient wealth provided from the coffers of the Reich, Moriarty would be well able to rebuild his criminal empire, with the added satisfaction of visiting a fiery revenge upon the homeland that has turned against him.'

'But if Moriarty has taken refuge in Germany, then he is already beyond our reach.'

'Recall, Watson, what Moriarty told us of the Nazi state: that he himself would be outside the protection of the law there. No, I do not believe he will allow himself to fall into the clutches of the Fuehrer.'

'In that case, where is he?'

'In a neutral setting where a deal may be negotiated, a place where all those who wish to keep their ill-gotten gains secure from scrutiny will find banks eager to do business with them. I am quite certain that Moriarty is at this moment in Switzerland making contact with agents of the Reich.'

'Holmes, that is a dire possibility. Can we intercept him in time?'

At that moment the phone rang. Holmes snatched it up, listened intently, then made a brief response before replacing the receiver.

'That was Mycroft. A plane is ready for us even now,' he informed me with satisfaction. 'If you would pack a bag with all possible haste, our quarry awaits.'

29

A CHALLENGE ACCEPTED

The two Germans seated in a corner of the rustic tavern in the Swiss village of Meiringen nursed their drinks with growing signs of impatience. Finally the larger of the two, whose short-cropped hair seemed to bristle with irritation, drained the last of his beer and slammed the empty stein down hard on the tabletop. He uttered a guttural curse and growled, 'Where is he? He is late!'

His slender, bespectacled companion winced slightly. He was clearly anxious that they should not draw attention to themselves. 'Rest easy, my friend,' he urged. 'You know the English.'

He moved to lay a calming hand on the other man's brawny shoulder only to draw back when the latter rounded on him with a glare of such fury it might have put a regiment to flight. He was about to order more drinks when the tavern door swung open and a bulky figure in a military greatcoat stepped across the threshold.

With a sharp hiss the bespectacled man captured his companion's attention and pointed out the newcomer with a subtle flick of his finger.

The stranger took a moment to glance around the busy room, then, catching sight of the two Germans, he came straight towards them with a determined stride. Sitting down opposite them, he removed his cap to reveal a head of brown hair which, like his bushy moustache, was flecked with grey.

'Herr Goltz, Herr Faber, I apologise for the delay. These Swiss roads!'

He spoke excellent German, but with an obvious English accent.

The larger German, whom he had addressed as Goltz, pushed his stein aside and leaned forward. 'You are Moran?'

The Englishman nodded. With his distinctive moustache and the fact that his padded greatcoat gave him an appearance of bulk, he matched adequately the description they had been given.

'Where is the professor?' the bespectacled Faber inquired.

'Don't worry, he's close by,' the Englishman assured him.

'You have the proof?' Goltz demanded curtly.

The newcomer extracted a folded piece of paper from an inside pocket of his greatcoat and handed it over. Goltz opened it, squinted and passed it to his companion. On it was written a fragmentary part of a complex chemical formula.

'This looks correct,' Faber acknowledged. 'And the material?'

'With the professor in a safe place not far from here,' the Englishman answered. 'You have the payment?'

Goltz reached under the table and pulled out an attaché case. He snapped open the locks and displayed the contents to the Englishman – a small fortune in bearer bonds which would be accepted by any Swiss bank. When the man with the moustache reached to take it, Goltz slammed it shut and locked it.

'No,' he said, 'we will hold on to this until we are face to face with the professor and can make the exchange.'

The Englishman looked momentarily discomfited, but shrugged it off and reached for his cap. 'As you wish. There is a car waiting outside to take you to him.'

The three rose and walked out into a narrow street leading off the village square. A Daimler saloon waited there with a uniformed chauffeur at the wheel. The Englishman opened the rear door and ushered the two Germans inside where a shatterproof screen separated them from the driver. As soon as he closed the door the car pulled away.

What the passengers did not yet realise was that the doors and windows were all securely locked and that beneath their seat was a canister of soporific gas that would soon be doing its work.

Seated at one of the other tables, I had covertly observed the meeting from behind a local newspaper. Now I joined Sherlock Holmes outside and together we watched the chauffeur-driven car disappear round a corner.

'What will become of them?' I asked.

Holmes tugged away the false moustache that was the most uncomfortable part of his disguise. 'Oh, they'll wake up somewhere in the woods with a mild headache and without their precious case. We are on neutral ground, so we can't be caught harming any German nationals, however wicked their intent. The driver is one of our Swiss sympathisers who can't be connected to the car.'

'And there's been no sign of Moriarty or Moran?'

Holmes gave a frustrated shake of the head. 'It was fortunate that our OSS contacts in Bern were able to intercept the German messages forewarning us of this rendezvous. There was always the chance, however, that

Moriarty would become aware of our presence and keep a cautious distance.'

'Do you mean he might be watching us even now?' I couldn't help glancing around uneasily.

'Don't worry, old fellow.' Holmes gave me a reassuring clap on the back. 'He won't make his move in public. Let's go back to the hostel. I'm sure you'd enjoy a late lunch and I can get rid of this makeup.'

By the time he joined me in the small dining room of the Englischer Hof, my friend had restored his normal appearance. He hung his coat and scarf on a peg by the door and sat down opposite me at the neatly laid table. A pink-cheeked waitress brought us plates of pork sausages with *rosti* potatoes, cheese and salad, which we washed down with tankards of locally brewed beer. Once we had finished our meal Holmes lit a cigarette and contemplated the coils of smoke drifting through the air.

'So, Holmes, what will be Moriarty's next step?' I wondered.

'I always judged it unlikely he could be lured into any sort of trap,' Holmes mused, 'but I still hold out the hope that my mere presence will flush him out. I have dismantled his criminal organisation, brought ruin to his plans, and now I have cut off his intended means of finance. His desire for personal vengeance will be close to boiling point.'

'But, Holmes, the danger to you in such a stratagem . . .'

'Must be risked,' he stated firmly. 'Even without the last supply of phlogiston Moriarty would represent a menace to the interests of every decent society. With it he might yet incite horror on a global scale while setting himself up in a new base of operations beyond our reach.'

At this point a fair-haired boy of about ten years old entered the room, looked around and made his way to our table.

'You are Mr Sherlock Holmes?' he asked my friend diffidently.

'Indeed I am,' Holmes answered. 'What can I do for you?'

'A gentleman outside asked me to deliver this to you,' the boy explained, handing over a sealed envelope.

'Why, thank you,' said Holmes. I could see that the name Sherlock Holmes was indeed written on the envelope.

The boy shuffled his feet uneasily. 'The gentleman said you would pay me.'

'Watson, would you please?' said Holmes, reaching for an unused butter knife to slice open the letter.

I fished out a couple of coins for the boy who clutched them gleefully as he darted back outside. I saw Holmes pull out a single sheet of paper which he read with narrowed eyes.

'What is it, Holmes?'

He hesitated a moment then handed me the letter. I read it with a growing presentiment of danger.

Holmes, you have crossed me once again. It is now perfectly clear that my purposes cannot advance so long as you are free to interfere, nor can you rest easy so long as I am at large. I propose that we settle this matter for once and for all in a personal confrontation.

I shall await you on the cliffs above the Reichenbach Falls one hour from now. I trust you to come alone, for the sake of your honour and the safety of your friend the good doctor.
M.

'The Reichenbach Falls – I have heard them spoken of hereabouts as a spectacular piece of scenery,' I said.

'I doubt their picturesque charms are the reason Moriarty has chosen them for our final meeting,' said Holmes, taking the letter back and perusing it once more.

'But you surely can't mean to go!' I exclaimed. 'It's an obvious trap.'

Holmes folded the letter and put it in his pocket. 'Perhaps. It may, however, be my only chance to put an end to Moriarty before he can flee to a fresh lair in some remote corner of the globe.'

A chill ran down my spine as I recalled how at our first meeting with Moriarty, Holmes had declared his willingness to sacrifice his own life so long as he dragged the professor into oblivion with him.

I banged my fist on the table. 'No, Holmes, I absolutely forbid it.'

An amused twinkle came into his eye. 'Is that your advice as my doctor?'

'I see no reason for levity,' I retorted. 'The world cannot afford to lose you. Nor can I.'

Holmes leaned forward intently. 'I believe that Moriarty is quite genuine in his desire to settle matters between us man to man with no outside interference.

In such a struggle I estimate my chances to be quite reasonable.'

'I don't think Moriarty will be abiding by the Marquis of Queensberry's rules,' I said. 'He's as treacherous as a cobra and just as deadly.'

'It is as you say,' Holmes conceded, 'but I must take that chance. To do otherwise would be sheer cowardice.'

'Then take me with you,' I insisted. 'You must at least see the sense in that.'

'No, old friend. If I appear otherwise than alone, Moriarty is almost certain to have an escape route planned and would be gone before we can lay hands on him. You must stay behind.'

I could see that he was not to be swayed. 'In that case,' I said, 'will you at least take my pistol?'

I drew the gun from my jacket pocket and passed it to him under the table where no one would see.

'Very well,' said Holmes, accepting it. 'If it will make your mind any easier.'

'My mind is anything but easy,' I told him. 'But if you are not to be dissuaded from this reckless course of action, you will at least go prepared.'

He stood up, his back straight, his lean face set in an expression of fixed determination. 'If I am not to keep the professor waiting, I had best make a start,' he said. 'I believe it is a long, steep climb up the falls.'

I walked him to the door of the hostel and we exchanged a few final words of parting. Then I watched him walk away down the street with a resolute stride, marching towards whatever destiny awaited him at the Reichenbach Falls.

30

THE FINAL RECKONING

I, of course, had no intention of letting Sherlock Holmes face his malevolent adversary without my support. As I knew his destination, I reasoned that it would be a simple matter to follow while keeping out of sight and so be on hand at the end should he require my aid.

Once Holmes had passed out of view, I set off at a brisk pace for the Reichenbach Falls. Occasionally I would catch a distant glimpse of my friend up ahead and deliberately slacken my pace so that his keen eyes should not spy me transgressing his instructions.

Leaving behind the cheerful, well-ordered environs of the village of Meiringen, I began my ascent of the rough track that zigzagged steeply towards the head of the falls. On both sides of the path clumps of hawthorn crowded together while above me loomed shadowy stands of larch and pine.

Clouds were gathering over the surrounding peaks which cast their lengthening shadow down into the gorge below me. Ominously in the distance I could hear the thunderous crash of the waters. Rounding a difficult turn I caught my first glimpse of the falls high above, a tumultuous avalanche of grey.

The atmosphere was so heavy with menace that I was almost seized by an impulse to break into a run, to catch up with Holmes and beg him to turn back. I knew, however, that any interference from me would in all likelihood rob him of what might well be his only opportunity to capture that malevolent genius who had led us such a chase. I braced myself with the assurance that he was armed and so had a fighting chance of defending himself against whatever murderous danger might await.

I pressed on through parts of the track that were so choked with overgrowth that I had to fight my way through while repeatedly snagging my clothing on branches and prickly snares of bracken. I was at length obliged to halt in order to catch my breath and take my bearings.

Behind me lay a dizzying maze of twists and turns. Above me, cold mists eddied up from the turmoil of the falls. A few feet to the left of where I stood, a rugged, scree-covered slope dropped down into a deep fosse, the walls of which were jagged with rock, like the waiting maw of a fanged beast.

Pulling away from that sickening drop, I had scarcely taken another step when I heard a sudden movement behind me. Before I could turn, a thin length of leather whipped around my neck and was pulled tight by a pair of unseen hands.

Choking, I clawed at the noose with my fingers but could gain no purchase. The guttural voice of Colonel Sebastian Moran sounded in my ear. 'The professor expected that you'd come sneaking along after your pal Holmes,' he grated. 'He doesn't want anybody interfering. He wants Holmes all to himself.'

I wrenched myself to right and left in an effort to shake him off, but Moran yanked me backwards, heaving me off my feet so that I could gain no leverage against him.

I sagged in the grip of my adversary, my vision clouding with red.

'Not to worry, doctor,' Moran mocked me, 'Holmes will be joining you in the grave.'

Even as I began to black out, the threat against my friend was enough to spark in me a ferocious determination to survive. My mind cleared just long enough for me to recall Moran laid out in our infirmary in France back during the Great War. He had taken a bayonet wound that left him in crippling pain for weeks afterwards. In a moment of desperate insight I realised that so deep an injury would have left an indelible and sensitive scar on his brawny physique.

With only scant seconds of life left to me I remembered that he had been stabbed on the left-hand side of his lower abdomen. Mustering all the strength I had left, I drove my elbow hard into that vulnerable spot.

I was rewarded with an anguished howl of agony from Moran and a loosening of the leather garrotte that allowed me to tear it from his grasp and fling it away. I wheeled round to see him doubled over in blinding pain. Seizing my chance, I grabbed him by the shoulders and propelled him headlong towards the precipitous drop that bordered the path. With a forceful shove I sent him over the edge and he tumbled down the rocky slope into the darkness of the waiting gorge.

Even as I sucked in a grateful breath, I launched myself back up the slope. All that mattered to me now was to reach Sherlock Holmes in time to save him from whatever evil trap Moriarty had laid for him.

Professor Moriarty stood framed by a dank cloud of mist swirling up from the falls. He loomed large in a long, dark coat, his smooth face shadowed by a soft, wide-brimmed hat such as the local priests were accustomed to wear. One gloved hand rested on the head of a mahogany walking stick. In the other he gripped a gold pocket watch in an ostentatious show of impatience.

A flicker of movement among the trees below heralded the arrival of Sherlock Holmes. Leaning his weight on his stick, Moriarty flipped open the watch and consulted the dial.

'You are tardy, Mr Holmes.' He snapped the watch shut and slipped it back into his waistcoat. 'A few minutes more and I would have felt compelled to leave.'

Holmes cast a backward glance at the path behind him. 'I apologise if I have inconvenienced you. You will appreciate that the climb is not an easy one.'

Moriarty inclined his head. 'Quite so. You are armed, of course?'

Holmes touched a hand to the side pocket of his coat. 'Your invitation made no stipulation on that account, so yes.'

'As am I,' said Moriarty. 'But only as a precaution.'

Delicately, using only his thumb and forefinger, he drew a small pistol from an inside pocket of his overcoat. Dangling it before him by the butt, he said, 'I see you have played fairly and come alone, so I have no need of this. Gun-play is for common gangsters, not for men such as we.'

So saying, with a flick of his wrist he pitched the pistol over the edge and down into the swirling torrent. With narrowed eyes, Holmes eased his own revolver into view and levelled it at his enemy.

Moriarty emitted a cold chuckle. 'Really, Mr Holmes, do you seriously expect me to believe that you would shoot an opponent who has already disarmed himself? Why, you would as soon shoot me in the back without warning. No, I judge you to be a man of honour and expect you to act accordingly.'

Maintaining his guard, Holmes said thinly, 'You surely don't believe I will simply let you walk away.'

'I have no intention of walking away,' said Moriarty. 'As I stated in my letter, I wish to settle this matter between us for once and for all in a personal contest of strength and skill.'

Adjusting his grip on his stick, he used his other hand to open his coat and pivoted from side to side, inviting his adversary's inspection. 'As you can see, I have no other weapon than my bare hands and my unquenchable animosity towards you. So, are you prepared to engage in an even struggle?'

Holmes slowly lowered his gun. 'You believe it to be such?'

Moriarty shrugged. 'I am aware of your physical prowess,' he conceded, 'but I have made a study of certain techniques of hand-to-hand combat which should put us on an even footing. If you will allow me to make a further demonstration of good faith . . .'

He reached carefully into a pocket and withdrew a glass vial containing the last deadly sample of phlogiston. Setting it down on a nearby rock, he turned to Holmes once more. 'There. Whoever wins this battle will leave with the last of Price's incendiary formula. If you will dispense with that ugly weapon, then we can begin.'

Holmes cast a sharp eye over the vial. The virulent green of its contents assured him that it was genuine. Satisfied, he flung the pistol aside into the foliage out of reach. 'There, professor. Now let us have our final duel.'

'Final indeed,' said Moriarty with an icy smirk.

He half-turned as if to set his walking stick aside, but instead made a quick adjustment that opened up a trigger mechanism. When he raised the stick, Holmes found himself staring into the barrel of a cunningly disguised gun.

'For a man of such vaunted intellect,' said Moriarty, 'you are most pitiably naïve.'

Holmes faced him calmly. 'I have seen such a weapon before,' he said. 'It is capable of only one shot.'

'I assure you that is all I require. I am an expert marksman.'

Holmes raised a scornful eyebrow. 'Since my execution was always your intent, why the elaborate charade of fair play?'

Moriarty hefted his weapon and smiled. 'You will appreciate, Mr Holmes, that it was important to me to test the extent of your quaint standards of nobility.'

'And have I passed that test?'

'In a manner of speaking. My experiment is concluded. I have demonstrated that a man who clings to such outmoded values will always fall to the man who disdains them. In this case the fall is a literal one.'

He swung his weapon briefly towards the thundering cascade of the Reichenbach Falls.

Holmes said, 'You mean to send me over the edge?'

'I urge you to jump. The choice is yours, Mr Holmes – either perish dramatically beneath the torrent or be shot like a dog. Personally it would please me more to see you end your days as a suicide.'

Holmes took a careful step towards the brink and peered into the depths below.

'You are estimating your chances of surviving the fall, I suppose,' mocked Moriarty. 'I must tell you, they are slim indeed. Are you ready to make the plunge?'

Holmes began to unwrap his scarf. 'Might I first disencumber myself?'

'As you please.' The professor tilted his head nonchalantly. 'It will make no difference.'

Unknown to Moriarty, there was a lead weight bound up invisibly in one end of the scarf, turning it into a weapon with the potential to crack bones apart when wielded by a practised hand. As soon as he had unwrapped it from his neck, Holmes twisted about and, with a whip-like motion, sent the weighted end flying through the air at his foe.

Flinching, Moriarty loosed off a shot an instant before the missile cracked his cheek. The bullet creased the detective's skull and he dropped to the ground as though felled by a cosh.

With a shriek of pain and rage, the professor wiped the blood from his cheek with the back of his hand. He pulled the handle from his walking stick to reveal six inches of sharpened steel and threw the rest of it away. Straddling the body of his fallen adversary, he snarled, 'No more tricks, Holmes! No more games! This is the end for you at last!'

As he raised the dagger to strike his helpless victim, I burst from the trees, having finally found my way to the top of the falls. I flung myself at Moriarty and we grappled with a savage fury.

The professor's thin lips drew back to expose his sharp teeth in a grimace of insane hatred. As I shook the dagger out of his hand we staggered back and forth, striking and clutching. In the ferocity of our struggle we were blind to our surroundings and it was with a sickening shock that we lost our footing and toppled over the cliff edge.

Down we tumbled through the mist, head over heels in a dizzy swirl, while the hungry torrent roared all around us. Even as we plummeted to our doom, Moriarty's fingers clawed at my throat, striving to rend my flesh. I struck the water with a horrendous impact that jarred the breath out of me and was immediately sucked down into the churning cauldron. As blackness enveloped me, my last thought was that if I had saved the life of my dearest friend, then I had not died in vain.

I awoke to the sound of rushing waters close at hand. Blinking in the afternoon sun, I realised that I had been dragged up on to a rocky river bank and leaning over me in deep concern was Sherlock Holmes. Like me he was soaked through and there was a bloody gash along the side of his head where the bullet had struck.

'Holmes! Thank God! Thank God!' I panted.

'Whether or not our survival can be classed as miraculous I leave for others to debate,' he responded with a weary smile. 'But we are mightily fortunate to be alive.'

'How?' I asked. 'What happened?'

'The full story of my final confrontation with Professor Moriarty can wait for another time,' Holmes answered. 'When I shook off the impact of that bullet on my skull, the first thing I saw was the vial of phlogiston lying close by. I lurched over and grabbed it. Then when I turned I was shocked to see you and the professor going over the edge. As quickly as I could, I stripped off my coat and made a controlled dive into the falls. By minimising my point of entry I was just able to keep from blacking out, though I barely avoided being smashed against the rocks. It was a close-run thing, but I managed to grab hold of you and fight my way to the shore.'

'You took a terrible chance,' I gasped.

'No more than you had taken for me.'

'And Moriarty?'

Holmes shook his head. 'I caught a glimpse of his shattered body being carried off by the current. The world can rest easy on that score.'

I forced myself into a sitting position in spite of the painful protest of my limbs. 'So we can go home,' I murmured hopefully.

'There is one last thing to do,' said Holmes, rising to his feet and stepping to the river's edge. He produced the vial of phlogiston, removed the stopper and let the contents pour down into the rushing waters.

'Let's send it back to the devil,' he said, 'along with Professor Moriarty.'

The struggle will go on, Watson, for a pearl, a kingdom, perhaps even world dominion, until the greed and cruelty are burned out of every last one of us, and when that time comes, perhaps even the pearl will be washed clean again.

Sherlock Holmes, *The Pearl of Death*
(Universal Pictures, 1944)

AUTHOR'S NOTE

Professor Moriarty looms large in the mythology of Sherlock Holmes, even though in the original canon of stories he makes only a few brief appearances. The background of World War II offered an opportunity to expand this classic confrontation between the two arch-enemies, particularly as the role given to Moriarty here by the British government seems entirely fitting. It was also gratifying that the plot led logically – indeed inevitably – to the Reichenbach Falls.

Many readers will see at once that Hunterswood is a fictionalised version of the once secret – now famous – World War II decoding centre at Bletchley Park. Hunterswood is not intended to be in any way an accurate representation of the historical establishment and readers seeking the true story will be able to find many books on that fascinating subject.

While the deadly phlogiston featured in this novel is a piece of fiction, between the wars the Germans did indeed develop a form of chlorine trifluoride which they referred to as N-Stoff. It was found to be an effective incendiary weapon and poison gas, though sources disagree as to whether it was actually deployed.

My thanks go once again to my wife Debby, who edits my work with a constructive ruthlessness, to Kirsty Nicol for her invaluable assistance in researching the most abstruse subjects, and to Dr Toby Lipman for his advice on matters musical and medical. Dr David Cole-Hamilton provided scientific information, which I may have somewhat misused for the purposes of fiction.

I am also very appreciative of the support given to this reimagining of Sherlock Holmes by everyone at Polygon.

For more on these novels and my other projects, do visit my website at www.harris-authors.com.

R.J.H.